AIN'T QUITE WHAT I THOUGHT!

2

BY

MIRIKA MAYO CORNELIUS

Ain't Quite What I Thought! 2

AIN'T QUITE WHAT I THOUGHT! 2

This is a work of fiction. Names, characters, places and incidents are either products of the author's imagination or are used fictitiously. Any resemblance to actual events or locales or persons, living or dead, is entirely coincidental.

All rights reserved, including the rights of reproduction in whole or in part in any form.

ISBN: 0970851766

Copyright © 2013, Mirika Mayo Cornelius
An Akirim Press publishing

Ain't Quite What I Thought! 2

ACKNOWLEDGEMENTS

All glory, honor, praise and total worship to God Almighty, Jesus Christ and Holy Spirit.

For my loved ones – son, husband, parents, siblings, nieces, nephew and grandmother along with the rest of my family of relatives - I love you all, those both here and that have passed on. You mean so much to me.

To all fans of Ain't Quite What I Thought, this sequel, and my other written projects, thank you.
God bless you all.

Mirikacornelius.com

Ain't Quite What I Thought! 2

AIN'T QUITE WHAT I THOUGHT!

2

Ain't Quite What I Thought! 2

"Morning, baby," I stated excited as ever to be spending my very first night as Mrs. Stay Black at my new home with my brand new husband. It had only been one week since we'd been back from our honeymoon, and I was in full gear, ready to be the best wife that I could be. The breakfast, I'd already laid out for Black at the small, round kitchen table made for a bachelor. I woke up extremely early and made Black a huge omelet, fully loaded and cooked to perfection, having had much practice in the kitchen one full year before my legal name change.

Black came out of the room looking like the newly promoted manager that I wasn't accustomed to quite yet, but I had to admit – I liked it. The whole in control vibe gave him a swag that made me want to tackle his behind right back into the bed, but that wouldn't bring any money into the house, thus, I let him stroll his sexy butt to the table.

"Morning back to you, baby, and you know you don't have to jump right into this wifey thing so fast," he said, checking me out in the process. "You're putting the pressure on me to step my husband game up, so take a step back and play girlfriend some more. You know I like that. I'm not in a big rush to see you washing clothes and looking like an old maid. You're my wife. I don't want to work the sexy out of you, so relax a bit. We're in it for life. You have plenty of time to cook me meals. Save that energy," he stated, leaning in to give me a sexually charged kiss that nearly made my knees buckle. I'd heard people say that marriage took the umph out of the attraction, but my attraction to my man had only grown stronger since the I do's on the beach.

It was amazing how we went from being associates to friends and then to lovers, topping it off with a wedding ceremony! I was living in a dreamland come true considering all the crap that went wrong and nearly took our lives in the very beginning of it all. Black getting shot and me getting nearly stabbed to death over a false piece of love that I misconstrued as real love that ended up turning both our lives upside down. But then there was God, and He made everything alright. We survived and got another chance to turn things around.

"I'm not trying to put any pressure on you, babe," I responded, pinching him on his butt and giving a wink as I reached to grab him a fork from the drawer. "I just want you know that this good stuff is just the beginning, and I'm worth every single minute of it. And don't worry...I won't work myself too hard. Never that!" I joked. I was all for serving my man – to the extent that it didn't turn into maid service. I'd need a paycheck for that.

Truth was, I did have a lot to prove to Black, and it was far more than he had to prove to me. As far as I could think back to when I met him, he was the exemplary man, even when I paid him no attention. It was me who had a loose end, literally jumping in and out of bed with a married man, and that was when Black came full force into my life as the only one I could talk to about it. I was a full deck of wreck and a side order of sin, but Black took me anyway, even after I nearly got him killed. That fact alone made me owe him as much goodness from myself as I possibly could give him.

I once called it embarrassing, but to be much more honest about how I felt back then in my sneaking days, my life was a three-hundred and sixty degree nightmare on my own dang street! When I was sleeping with a married man, Tina's husband to be precise, I really thought I was doing something...thought I was fine and had to be sexing it the right way since her man was all over me, but I was wrong, dead wrong to be exact. The marks ended up permanent from when his wife went loon on me with the knife, leaving scars above my breast, while I laid in the hospital bed suffering from a previous attack from Andre' that left myself and Black for dead. I couldn't say I didn't deserve it because that wouldn't be fair, but I was seriously trying to let go of the adulterous relationship before that incident even happened! It was Andre' that wouldn't let go, and that was when his craziness got even crazier.

Stay Black reached over, ignoring the polished fork that I was handing him, pulling me into his space. "You don't have to prove anything to me. People mess up, baby. As long as you don't bring that in here with us, we're cool. I love you." He kissed me on the cheek and lips, then prepared to eat with a huge grin on his face as he planted himself into the chair. "And thank you for this mean omelet I'm about to swallow whole because I'm late."

He knew how to change the subject well. Fact was, he didn't like for me to drag the past into our present and future, especially when the both of us have healed physically while time was supposed to make the baggage heal emotionally as well as psychologically. There was just one major problem with that - sometimes the past was all I could think about. Even on the honeymoon, I found myself trying to prove in word and extra deeds that I wasn't that bad person my whole life, that it was just a small portion of my life, never once giving in to the fact that Black didn't care about it. All he cared about was me, and that, to me, was a new thing. I needed to get used to having that from a man other than my own flesh and blood father.

"Well, slop it down, and try to have a super day today at work." I watched as Black, with his dreadlocks pulled back in a neat band, shove three bites of the omelet into his mouth, cheeks packed and orange juice glass filled to the rim. There was no room for him to drink, and I hoped to God he didn't choke because life insurance, we had none – yet. Getting that was on the top of the list though being that our young lives were nearly cut short a year ago.

As he shoveled the food down, he didn't even take a full swig of his orange juice before he handed me the glass back while I kissed his closed mouthed, omelet lips as he ran out the door in his dapper suit. I followed his every footstep until he got into the car. There I stood as his wife in the driveway, barefoot with a glass of orange juice in my hand – just not pregnant - and I wanted to be, but like Black said, we still had a lifetime.

Taking my time, walking on my tip toes back inside the house after picking up a newspaper from the grass, I immediately scraped up the last little bit of omelet I left for myself in the pan and got on the telephone. It was crunch time. Crunch time was when I had to call my girls so that I could get in with the fill in, find out what I missed while I was away and vice versa. They vowed that they wouldn't call me until I called them because they figured there would be a huge don't disturb us sign on my door and on the voicemail greeting. Well, they were right. The honeymoon came right back to the house, and the love making went into overtime. I dang near caught a hernia.

It was Tanya I would call first because she wasn't working. The job she had that was paying her part-time pay for fulltime work laid her off. The last time I spoke to her was at the wedding, and she was actually looking like she was over the drama and into the dollars, trying to make a better life for herself and kids without a man. She could've been putting on airs for me since the mood of the wedding day was strictly to keep me happy, but outside of that, I really wanted her to be in a good place in her life, especially with the new baby added to the crew.

As the phone rang, I sat on the couch that I can't wait to get rid of. It was Black's couch from our pre-marriage slash dating days, and there was absolutely no way I was going to spend more than one year with this furniture in the house with us. Sure, it was cute when we dated to see that my man had his décor down, and even though he said he really didn't date much, what man wouldn't say that? I only imagined Sue, Silly, Dopey and Dizzy lying down and smooching with my husband back in the day on this same furniture. If I imagined it, then it was highly possible that Black had his memories, too, when he sat down, walked by or even breathed in the leather. Therefore, the couches were on the way out sooner rather than later. The new mattress was delivered yesterday. We broke that sucker in great!

"Well, well, well, would you look at what my caller ID brings to the phone! What's up, girl?" Tanya hollered, either happy to hear my voice or happier to be closer to gettting the goods on how my honeymoon went.

"Yeah, chica. How are you and the children with the newborn?" I asked, immediately diving in, wanting to be certain that she's still on the straight and thinking narrow path. I thought back to when she was about to stab her then man and newborn baby daddy to death and hoped to God she was doing well without him still. Tanya had a way of putting out the good crap and hiding the bad crap until things explode. Snooping was unlike me, therefore, I did it the less overt and long routed kind of way by starting with the kids.

"All of us are good," she sang happily, almost too happy.

"Am I missing something, Tanya?" I asked as I crossed my legs and leaned back on the sofa. "You sound happier than I am, and I'm the one who just married the man of my dreams and had the best boom boom in the bedroom ever."

"Shut up! Was it good, Jeena?"

"Better. But don't change the subject. You heard me. You sound like..."

"Like what, Jeena?" she interjected.

"Like you got a man... and not just any old man, but a good one."

There was complete silence. I knew it. She was in another relationship just that fast after giving birth. I wondered if she even lasted the sixty days they say not to have sex afterward. More than likely, whoever this dude was split the seam after sitting on the sidelines.

"I got something to tell you."

"I already know that, Tanya. The excitement is racing through your pores."

"Now I know what you're thinking, but this one, this one, Jeena, you won't guess at all. I'm not telling you yet because I want this to happen face to face."

"When?"

"I'm gonna call Parri, and we'll come over. She's been dying to talk to you anyway, so she can swing by and pick me up."

"Is she off today?"

"No, but she said she would get sick to get off work whenever you gave the word."

That was Parri. Ready for anything, and if she wasn't ready, she made things go her way anyway. This was great for me because I didn't tell them I was quitting my job, and I didn't have crap to do today but wait on them to come over. I couldn't wait to see them, so I would keep the news of my unemployment to myself until the big reveal later.

"Well then go ahead and let her know, and I'll be here. Not going anywhere soon, except maybe to the store down the street to pick up some snacks."

"That's a bet, married lady. See you later!"

"Bye." I hung up the phone, got up from the chair, and skipped back to the bedroom to get ready. As I passed by the mirror, the sparkle from my wedding band caught my eye. I was in love. The ring was fantastic, but it was more than that. I was really in love, and there was nothing my ex Andre' nor his wife could do about it either. They were both going to rot in prison like molded pieces of bread, and I felt so free as I searched the closet to get ready for the rest of my day. That was when it fell.

I'd forgotten about it during the honeymoon because I didn't want it to ruin the atmosphere that Black and I wanted which was romantic, fun and worry-free. Unfortunately, as the white card laid face down on the closet's floor, the fun and romance left my mood, leaving only worry behind. As I kneeled down on the floor, my oversized pink shirt covered my knees as it rubbed across the decorated edge of the card that was left for me at the end of the wedding ceremony. Then, I finally picked it up and flipped it over, hoping that the same way I brushed it from my life during the honeymoon, it would disappear again. To my nightmare, it was very real, and it read the same thing –

<u>"Congratulations, but this shit ain't over".</u>

As I stood up with the card in my hand, thoughts raced through my mind about how I hid it from Black in the limo, lying to him basically just so that he wouldn't have to deal with me and the baggage that came along with me. He'd already defended me once, nearly costing him his life, and I yearned to make things right. Therefore, I hid the note from him, brushing it off as if it were just a very simplistic congrats to the married couple. In reality, it was the most dreaded threat to hit my happy home the very first day of our marriage.

Instead of preparing to finally tell Black about the threatening card, I continued in my denial, placing it in a location where only I would look and where it had no chance of falling into plain view – the small drawer where I keep my feminine products. There wasn't a chance in the middle of hell Black or any other man would snoop in that area. The thought did cross my mind to rip it up and toss it into the dumpster outside, but if something did pop off, I wanted evidence. With a flip of the coin though, I didn't think much of anything else happening because how could it? Both Andre' and Tina were in lock up, right?

"Forget about this, Jeena," I told myself closing the drawer and taking another glimpse of myself in the mirror hanging on the wall. "The only thing left from your past is this scar," I stated, taking off my shirt. "And even though you don't have your natural boobs anymore, these fake ones are working for Black just fine." After standing tall and proud, I slumped over, dropping backwards onto the bed to stare at the ceiling. I started to rub on the top of my breast where Tina stabbed me, missing my heart by a fraction. The skin was healed up, but lumpy, like a minor keloid. It wasn't bad, but it was a painless, unattractive reminder of that one thing Black wanted me to forget – my former life as a psycho's mistress.

The word mistress sounded so glamorous. When someone thought mistress, the thought leaned more toward a *kept* woman on the side. I was more like a *keeping* woman, making great leaps and bounds to keep him in my life versus the other way around. Giving him the key to my condo wasn't the brightest idea. Maybe it was the bushiest, but not the brightest at all. No, instead of mistress, I was more like the jump *way* off. I got minimal out of the situation such as a bad reputation, a stab wound, beat down, and really, I was just tired. Stay Black was right. I needed to forget everything and learn to live life for a good future.

"Forget this mess, Jeena. You have to. Everything is going to be fine. Trust this. As long as you do well, you get well." At least that was what Faith told me from this scripture in the Bible. There was a conversation between God and killer named Cain who murdered his own flesh and blood brother, and God said something *like if you do well, won't you be accepted? But if you do evil, sin will meet you at the door and it's desire will be for you.* I took that as a command to do well so sin will leave you alone and better things will come your way. That was what I decided, and so far, that was what I got, hoping the consequences of the past deeds were over and done.

By the time it was noon, there was a knock at the door plus heavy ringing of the doorbell. That was no one other than Tanya, Parri, or both of them as planned. When I peered through the peephole, I was absolutely right. Both of them were break dancing at the front door, doing the wave, looking like the female versions of stuck in the past and the eighties divas. I was happy to see them, so I spared the cars that passed by the parade on the porch and let them inside. As soon as our eyes met, we screamed at the top of our lungs like little kids.

"Jeena!"

"Parri!" I screamed first and then grabbed them both simultaneously. "Tanya! What's up, ladies?" The both of them looked like their next step was going to the gym or for a good walk because they came over in everything stretchy, and I was right. Instead of chilling at the house, they had exercise in mind.

"We're about to get you out of the house because we don't want you to turn into an old maid too fast, ain't that right, Tanya?"

Tanya agreed with a stay fit and sexy comment. "Damn right, so come on out there, change those house maid jeans you got on and let's shake some extra blood in those thighs because your man will be home tonight..."

Parri interjected, "And he wants you to stretch!"

This was the first time that either one of them had stepped foot inside what used to be just Black's home. As their eyes wandered, I watched. Those two literally stood back to back, cutting their eyes around at all the black that blended with all the rest of the black in the house.

Without saying much at all, tangling with under their breathing moans, Parri and Tanya stared at one another with the straightest faces topped with the droopy eyes look. Then, while holding their expressions, they trace the black air back to me, and I looked back at them with the explanatory facial motions stemming from the crinkle of my eyebrows.

"I know, it's all black down, but that's gonna change, ladies. The queen is officially half of this castle, and until we purchase another spot, color will reign in on this parade really soon."

"Well, hallelujah," Parri stated as she peeped down the hallway. "Oh heck no."

"Heck yeah," I responded, knowing exactly what she saw.

"A strobe light in the hallway and black power portraits lining the walls?" Parri took it all in and then busted out laughing, amazed at the depth of Stay Black's ethnic ties to the past. "Doesn't he know that half this wall should be of the Caucasian breed?"

"Ha, ha, really funny, Parri. You know he strictly identifies with his African American-ness," I responded jokingly. That was one thing about Black – he loved being black and would have it no other way. At the same time, he didn't defame his white side either. He was just as proud of that side except when he looked in the mirror, what he saw was a black man, the same as his father, looking back at him. His admiration for his father was unsullied, and he leaned to him much.

"I see that. I really see that," she continued, "now that I'm in here with all my flesh and blood." She sat down on the couch next to me. "So, how was the flesh and the blood, if you get me?" Parri cut her eyes to Tanya who winked and slid over to the other side of me, leaving me sandwiched between them.

I crossed my legs with whatever small bit of room they left me and started to wish I'd eaten onions and garlic so I could've stunned their wide open nostrils with my breath when I started talking, but my dish of choice wasn't an option this particular morning. Besides that, I wasn't going to lie, I was ready to deliver the goods, and boy was it good!

"Okay, okay, okay!" I started with a big smile creeping across my face as I fell back into the couch, yanking the pillow from behind me and shoving it into my face. Parri yanked it off my face while Tanya grabbed my cheeks like she would snatch them off if I didn't give her all the details of what married sex feels like. At that point, I had the upper hand as I slid from in between them and watched them huff, puff and drip like little strung out puppy dogs waiting to slob down all the information of what went down my hotel room with Black all week long. I began my story.

The honeymoon started with Stay Black lifting me out of our limo. We'd already moved our things into the hotel where we would make love from sun down to sun up the day before the wedding because we didn't want to waste any time nor have any interruptions. It was all we could do to keep our hands off of each other after we decided a while back that we would wait to make love. Shoot, two days prior to the wedding, we almost did it in the parking lot! My body was fried after all the ceremony planning, and I immediately needed to be hosed down by Stay Black's good loving. All I got before marrying Black was super stimulating body massages, which were nothing less than the freaking bomb, and the only thing I was able to give him were body teases where I would put on some sexy body spray and look fabulous while learning how to prepare excellent cuisines that filled his gut. The saying was that a tasty meal was the way to a man's gut and then to his heart, but I was really taking a stab at it satisfying his sexual cravings, too. What was so good about our courtship was that we were in it together, same goal, same soul, all the way to the altar.

After getting settled into the hotel room, it was a minute before I was able to face him with my new breasts which were reset and designed six months before the wedding. I had that post traumatic slice me up syndrome derived from Andre's wife, Tina, and I had to come to grips with living with the scars for the rest of my life. When Black got me inside the hotel, after helping me out of my gown, I was so paranoid that I didn't turn to face him. Heck no! I wasn't comfortable yet in my own skin, my own stretched skin, though the rest of my confidence, my performance confidence, was on point so I needed the lights off pronto! That was why I darted to the bathroom to freshen up. Sure, it was the normal thing to do right, freshen up before the big masquerade that was coming under the sheets, but I was afraid of being sexy with my extra scars. Up until that moment, we'd never had intercourse, and it mattered big time how I felt about myself, let alone how he saw me raw, uncut and naked.

Black ended up loving the fear out of me, though. When I came out of the bathroom, he loved the big, ugly scar on my breast and all, making me feel like I was the most breath taking woman on the planet as he laid me on the bed and proceeded to increase my heart rate. His hands felt all over me as he started kissing me on my legs, from the bottom of my ankles all the way up to my inner thighs. I was heated from the time his mouth touched my skin, so much so that all the blood in my body took a detour to my vagina like a rushing river. It was pulsating, like she was starving and ready to eat, and Black was getting ready to fill her up.

He licked me everywhere, and I mean everywhere. My high was just beginning, but he would soon take me even higher. The marriage bed...wow...I'd waited too long for it. True love, and sex never felt so right. Black lifted me so high in his arms as he stood up on the bed, that if I raised my hands, I could grab the ceiling. With my back against the wall, there was nowhere for me to go, but where he was taking me as he made love to my lips, neck, shoulders, and even my breasts – those brand new breasts. What scar? We'd already had our ride or die moment, and it was time for me to ride again – on top of my man.

As I satisfied Black like he'd hopefully never been satisfied before because I was just magnificent like that about the task at hand, I enjoyed being Mrs. Black for the first time. We did it every which way that we possibly could, and the thing about it was, we didn't speak one word to each other. We'd already done too much talking and not enough action prior to the ceremony, so voices were on mute and moans were on blast.

Black was sexy. Every inch of him hollered *oh yeah, Jeena, you hit the jackpot!* I'd been all over a man built like this before a few times in my past, but with Stay Black, this was legally and spiritually all mine, and of what was mine, I took full advantage. As I counted his abs with my tongue and lips, his skin reminded me of a freshly unwrapped, chocolate covered candy apple with nuts, my favorite junk food with good fruit in the middle. Delightful. Marriage...could it get any better than this? Just when I asked that question, it did. We went from the bed to the shower for the continuance of the marriage sex.

If Black and I were to have engaged in shower sex before marriage, well, I would have been too concerned about my hair getting wet and out of order but not that night. All hell was about to break loose on my strands, but I could have cared less. His naked body was on mine, and my fingertips gripped his back as the shower head poured water down on the both of us as I lightly rested on the bathtub rail, and he went in.

It was the flippin' bomb! If I wasn't already saved from sin and devoted to trying to walk my best walk before God every day even with slight to sometimes gaping mishaps, I would have cussed him out it felt so good, but instead I swallowed the curse words, replacing them with my very first words while in the middle of this obsessing sexual encounter with my husband, "Have mercy!" It was quite weird, but that was the most honest thing I could think of to replace all the other hell bent words that didn't exactly describe this technically God approved moment that felt so erotic that it needed some forgiveness! Black was going in, too, making his preacher daddy proud I could only assume because his dad was the one that emphasized having a great sex life. As Black did his thing, I got my I do's worth. After we finished, we went to bed wet, sexually fulfilled...

<u>And On An Amen.</u>

"What?" I asked, finishing my honeymoon story.

Parri and Tanya sat together on the leather couch, gripping the pillows with their mouths drooping open. Then, Parri finally cleared her throat to speak. Tanya, on the other hand, started sucking her teeth and rubbing her tongue all around her mouth like a lost hound.

"You have got to be freaking kidding me." She leaned over and tapped Tanya on her leg, never taking her eyes off of me. Then she stated in a low tone that seeped from the side of her mouth. "Ain't a man on this earth ever held me up on a bed so I could touch the damn ceiling."

"Nope, me either," Tanya responded, slanting her eyes over at Parri like they were about to gang up on me. "She's a damn lie. There's not a man in this universe playing no balancing act on a bed with you in the air...unless that was a hard ass bed!"

"Made of concrete," Parri agreed. "Got my ass jealous just that quick. I knew I should've gotten married a long time ago."

I couldn't believe those hating behind friends of mine. Dang! "And no, the bed wasn't made of concrete. Black did a slow and easy stroke when he lifted me..."

Tanya got up quickly and cut me off. "That's e-damn-nough, Jeena. We get the point. Taking the junk too far now, but thank you because I also have some news to let you in on.

"So spit it out, Tanya," I demanded anxiously. Obviously, Parri already had the beans spilled in her lap, so it was my turn.

Tanya reached inside her pocket and pulled out an engagement ring. "I'm getting married!"

"To who?" I asked, so stunned that I nearly choked on my own spit.

"Tony," she hesitated with a fuzzy smile. She turned to look at Parri who then turned to look into the kitchen, and then

Tanya, having no choice, stared back into my non-blinking eyes. "Yeah," she continued, rubbing her hands in between her knees nervously, "Remember Tony, Jee?"

We ended up over at Tanya's apartment as soon as possible, not because we wanted to go over, but because she wanted me and Parri, well, me especially, to get reacquainted with Tony, the father of her latest newborn baby whose name by the way was Toni with an I. Tanya really wasn't as stupid as she came off to be, but no matter how hard I tried, I couldn't place my finger on why she was acting so dumb at this moment in her life. Sure, I had my blinding spells of dumbness on a not so often basis, but her stuff just continued to go on and on like an annoying buzz, almost fly-ish.

When we got into the apartment, I could tell things were on the up and up with her. First thing was that she'd moved, but the main thing was that she'd gathered everything new, from the kitchen table to the furniture we sat on. The last time I saw the décor in her home, she was throwing it at Tony while I was lifting her then pregnant self off of him. She was inches from stabbing him with a homemade shank, but she never set foot in the jailhouse, thanks to him and her mom and most of all my merciful God in heaven Whom gives people more than a second chance.

Anyway, as I glanced around the living room, Tony the terrible was absolutely nowhere to be found. Meanwhile, Tanya sat in front of us like we...or I...was supposed to be ecstatic about the engagement. Parri lounged back, fluffed pillows and all, appearing fairly comfortable and that was probably because she didn't care one way or another. If I knew Parri as well as I thought I did, I knew she had something to say, and she was awaiting the right time to say it. She got her wish, too, because in walked Tony with the all of the kids, minus his blood daughter Toni.

"Anybody ever told you that you're crazy as hell, Tanya?" Parri finally blurted out now that everyone in the room, namely Tony, could come to his own defense.

"Parri!" Tanya exclaimed, standing up to greet her children. Then she started gritting her teeth together while moaning under her breath, "Don't do this, Parri, not now. If you have something to say, say it to me, not in front of..."

"Hey, ma! Daddy took us to the park."

Daddy? I twisted my neck back toward the front door to watch all the kids run inside with...their daddy.

"Auntie Jeena!"

"Hey, babies! Lemme count...one, two, three, four, five...yep all here and in order." As I embraced them, or stood there as they encapsulated me, I glanced at Tanya, and she assumed I gave her the eye because I didn't see the newest member of the family.

"Oh, baby Toni is with mom today."

"She can't be serious," Parri mumbled under her breath because she knew exactly why I'd looked at Tanya so hard – the kids calling Tony daddy.

"Well look who's here. Long time no see, Jeena." Then, he looked over at Parri for a split second. "Don't I know you? You look familiar."

Parri pretended to not hear him at all as she continued to stare at her shoe, so Tanya interjected quickly to diminish the tension.

"Tony, so you do remember Jeena from way back, right?"

Way back? I refrained from commenting. Try just some months ago, three to be exact. Tanya was strolling around about to bust with his baby in her womb when I caught them together. We all spoke, but there was nothing to the conversation that would have led me to believe that those two were back together and about to get hitched. Even at the wedding, Tanya didn't let on one single thing about it or him. What a strong secret she kept!

"Kids, go back in the room now," Tanya continued

"Auntie Jeena, do we have an uncle now named Stay?"

Despite the fact that I had no idea if Black was going to claim these creatons, I still responded affirmatively, "Yes, you have an uncle named Stay, and my last name is Black now."

"Y'all can just call her Auntie Stay Black," Tony said out the crack of his butt, and I didn't know butts like his could talk until that moment. The kids thought his little comment was hilarious, but before I had the chance to lose all of my new found and hard at work religion, Tanya rushed up and corrected him – fast!

"It's still Auntie Jeena to you guys, now go back there in the room like I said! Don't know what to laugh at! Tony, be nice." She grabbed the gremlin's hand and walked him over to the loveseat to sit by her, and my whole entire inside wanted to vomit all over his unshaven face. He slapped her butt before she sat down, and I was hoping some doo doo smeared off on his hand. Unfortunately, that was only a distant wish never to happen.

It was grossly obvious that Tanya wanted to continue this dreadful meeting with more upsetting news while Tony sat beside her, and she did. I personally didn't have time for the drama between him and what had to be a heavily sedated Tanya to even consider marrying a guy she caught in her bed with another woman while she was pregnant. One thing I did know was that I wasn't gonna go shank and stab stopping the next time he went AWOL with some other woman.

"Being that you and Parri are my best friends ever, I wanted to get the both of you together at the same time to ask you if you like to be my matron and maid of honor at my wedding?"

"You ready to go because I have to go and play sick at home since that's the excuse I gave my job to get off today?" Parri rudely interrupted, gravely serious about leaving Tanya buried in her stupid request as she sat there with Tony while he looked like a short side of sloppy. Parri and I both had our justified reservations about him from the start, and I couldn't say that I was any better than he was because when I met him, I was doing my dirt, too. However, wrong was wrong, and he did that wrong to my girl Tanya while she had his baby in her belly.

Parri stood up in the middle of Tony's attempt to check her at being so hostile. "Hey, girl, don't do that shit. My lady here is trying to make a decent request of you two and all you do is act like you're better than me – like your crack don't stink every once in a while."

Parri's back was already turned toward him when he started to shout, but when he mentioned her crack, she about faced, not addressing him but instead, she addressed Tanya.

"Tell your man that I wash my crack unlike his little slut monkeys on the side, and it's a crack that he'll never creep into, that's for sure." Then she winked at Tanya to reinforce that she was still cool with her, but just not with him. After that, she glanced at me. "Are you coming?"

"Parri!" Tanya screamed, "Sit back down!" Tears started to gush from her eyes and her bottom lip started to quiver, so instead of getting up from my uncomfortable seat, I shook my head at Parri which resulted in her sitting back down...to pick her nails.

"Look, Tanya," I stated, shoving Parri's leg. Sometimes she could be so overtly obnoxious, but in the end, once hind sight comes in clearly, she'd be the one that told the truth each time. "Yes. Yes, I will definitely be your matron of honor, but I can't lie to you, Tony," I turned my eyes toward him. "We have to get used to you being around. If Tanya loves you, then she loves you, and I'll respect that."

"Damn right because I don't." Parri chimed in.

"Parri!" Tanya yelled once again, well aware that Parri was going to say what she had to say, and that would be the end of it.

"Once a dumb dude, always a dumb dude...unless Jesus taps him is what I say," Parri continued to justify her forwardness which Tony wasn't accustomed to at all.

Instead of Tony getting up from his seat to get down and dirty, he leaned back in his seat, placing Tanya atop his lap. "Now that we got a matron, kick that other broad out my spot, Tanya, before I have to do some shit I'll regret."

"Oh, now this nigga crazy. Let's go, Jeena." Sure, Parri said that, but she was barely moving off the chair, and her voice wasn't shaken. Instead, she spoke monotone as she stared Tony

29

directly in his eyes, continuing to taunt him in a majorly sarcastic way. "Come on, Jeena. This is a scary mug in front me. Start the car up, girl. He's coming." Then, she thumped my leg with her finger. "He must have arthritis because he's slow at doing that regretful shit that he said he was gonna do five seconds ago."

"Somebody should slap your ass." Tony was now angry, and he was getting the purest Parri in her finest of hours.

"I agree," Parri snapped back. "And the man that does will catch a handful of nice ass and love it. Too bad it won't be you because I don't play that ass grabbing bull..."

At that, Tony nearly shoved Tanya on the floor, and I did what I decided I wouldn't do which was jump in the middle. Parri remained seated with a smile on her face wishing Tony would slap her - and on the left cheek, too - which didn't help the situation, and Tony fumed as Tanya grabbed his arm. I shoved his body backwards as hard as I could, not because I wanted to fight, but he was strong as ever. My own shove ended up shoving me backwards!

"She's not coming! Get her out my spot now!"

"Oh I'm coming, just not as her maid so I won't have to help her cater to your ass during the ceremony. I'll be sitting right on a pew looking at you, I mean, your sorry ass."

"You had to do that," Tanya yelled as Tony punched the wall, going down the hallway. I grabbed Tanya to calm her back down, and Parri just shrugged her shoulders.

"You know I'm gonna say the shit, Tanya, and you better say the same shit to me if I'm about to marry a damn extreme unsaint. I'm not perfect by any means, but I would want to at least marry someone that could help enhance my person. Damn! Is that too much to do, Tanya?"

"He's my baby's father, Parri, dog!" Tanya complained, huffing and puffing at the same time while I rub my forehead with my index and middle finger trying hard to scrub away the stress of the moment. "And you don't know him like that either for you to come at him that way."

"Your baby's father? Is that the reason for the matrimony?" Parri finally stood back up and looked around the entire room. She even picked up a magazine and looked underneath it before slamming it back down on the coffee table. "Well where are all the other baby daddies? You gonna marry them, too?" After picking a piece of lint from her shirt, Parri continued, "And you're right. He doesn't know me nor I him like that. The only person he has to know is you. Do you see his ring on my finger?" She looked down at her finger and then back at us. "I wouldn't marry a temperamental misfit like that anyway. Ain't nothing worse than an angry ass cheater."

"Okay that's enough, Parri."

"What, Jeena? It's her ceremony, damn, and he's mad? Why does he even care who her maid or matrons are as long as he has his boys backing him up."

"Tanya didn't ask for our lecture about who she chose to marry. Besides that, you could have held off telling her all of how you felt away from Tony. Now she has to go try and fix some stuff that you did." As I examined the stressed out demeanor suffocating Tanya, she pulled away from my arm, glaring at Parri.

"You always pick the wrong time, Parri, and you do the shit purposely. That's gonna stop."

"Someone had to say it because fantasy isn't how we are supposed to live," Parri explained, singing the word live in a high register. Then she rolled her eyes at both me and Tanya. "That same fantasy jive already got the both of you in trouble more than once." Then she stopped talking after realizing that she'd stepped on both our toes. Tanya and I stared at her bare faced and in awe, and she continued apologetically. "I'm sorry. My bad. I love you two, but sometimes if you don't see straight, I feel like I have to be the one to slap the hell out of you before you see the damn eye doctor. Save you some time and money." Then, she turned to yell down the hallway. "Sorry, Tony!" Parri then glanced back at Tanya who was literally dismayed at the apology. "You can come back out now!" she yelled as Tanya fell onto the chair with her head hung inside the palms of both her hands, the engagement ring appearing less solid as was the relationship.

Parri and I stared down the hallway, awaiting the return of Tony, and it never happened. Tanya, on the other hand, kept her head buried in sorrow without speaking a word to either one of us. When I did try to say something, all I got was a finger pointing to the door.

"Go."

"Tanya, I'm your maid, okay. Maid I am." Parri was a lot too late.

"Go, Parri," Tanya fumed.

"Seriously?"

"Parri, bye!"

Tony finally walked up the hall with a cigarette in his mouth and a grin. "You heard her."

"I don't need your extra after I already apologized to you, okay? Swallow the cigarette and cough up a lung. I'm sorry, Tony. There, ya see," she pointed to all her grinning, white teeth. "I'm not crying. Get a grip and stop whining. I say what's on my mind all the time, and it doesn't mean I hate you. You just dogged my girl out, and I don't like you for it. Simple."

"Well, take that simple ass of yours to the door."

"See, Tanya." she said. "He's always on another woman's ass. Now it's my simple ass again!" she complained while stressing the words simple ass.

I was already on my way out the door, unwilling to sit through anymore of the horror of the house. Parri knew better than to behave like she did, but we were so used to her doing it that we tolerated it each and every time. No matter how right she may have been the many times in our lives, she wasn't exactly tactful or respectful in her delivery most times. I did notice that she was getting much worse with her whole attitude overall, and I blame myself and Tanya for that because we allowed it instead of cutting her short.

I was already at the car when Parri came strolling out the door, waving good-bye to the kids who were busy pointing out of the window at her like they heard everything that was said. When I entered the car, I pulled down the visor and locked the door.

"I should make her jog all the way back to my house," I expressed to myself.

"Girl, let me in," she said, tapping the passenger's side window. Although I was hardcore for a second, that crap went out the window as I unlocked the door. She hopped inside.

"You were dead wrong." I pulled out of the driveway, but ended up coming to a screech after nearly hitting a kid on a bike. "Lord, have mercy!"

"How was I dead wrong? Maybe wrong, but not dead wrong. Wasn't a thing lethal about what I said. If anything, it brought life to the situation at hand."

"It's not what you said but how you said it, Parri. You know that, so don't act stupid. You feel too safe saying things to people that hit them in the gut. What if he was to get up and slap the skin off of your face just then?"

"Well, they'd have been slapping the skin of his ass in prison."

"And see...stop that, Parri. You're too sarcastic and angry acting. Maybe it's *you* that needs a man."

"Me?"

"You heard me. You jealous?"

"Girl, if I didn't love you and myself, I would wreck this car with you in it while I jump out for saying some mess like that. Jealous of who? Them things back at that apartment?"

"There you go again. Things, Parri? That's Tanya and Tony. I don't like him either, but I told him in another way. You're just out with it."

"That doesn't make me wrong either."

"Parri, you called the man an unsaint. Who says that? What is that?"

"Me...and to answer the second question - him."

It was no use. She wasn't going to get it, and even if she did get it, she wasn't going to admit it. Something was going on with her, and whatever it was, it was worsening by the weeks that go by. For instance, while I was planning my own wedding with my mom's assistance, Parri was on the sidelines being a really strong support, however, she would sometimes toss out a snide remark from the sides of her lips. One of those comments pertained to why would I want to marry a flower boy? I was thinking, are you for real? That flower boy just saved my life. After she asked that ignorant question, she kind of walked away and started doing her own thing, not really even waiting on me to address her question with a response. She was really callous, but I let it go, attributing her funky mouth to hormones.

Instead of carrying on the conversation about her drought-free mouth, I asked Parri to stop inside my old condo with me. I was supposed to be meeting the new tenant, which by the way, I'd forgot to mention to Parri that I was quitting my job.

"So you haven't met her yet?"

"No, not yet," I responded, nearly wrecking when I turned the corner.

"Jeena, now, you either drive right or let me on the wheel so I can steer. The curb isn't the street, boo," she laughed while holding on to the seat.

"My bad, Ri," I giggled, holding on tight to the wheel. "Listen though, did I tell you that I'm quitting my job?"

"Quitting? Why?"

"I figured the money coming in from the tenant would supply me with enough funds, since mom and dad paid it off for me when I got stabbed as a feel bad for my daughter gift. Because of that, I decided to try to open my own business, get some things going to see if I can live outside of the big, huge workforce jungle for a while."

"What type of business are you about to delve into, Jeena? Wait, let me guess," she stated fixing her hair in the side mirror. "No, I can't guess. Tell me."

"An interior designer." I glanced over at her, and she was still looking straight ahead as if I'd said nothing. "Parri? Did you hear me?"

"Yeah. I'm just picturing it in my head, and I love it. I must admit, you do have a flair for décor after looking at all those books and stuff. I should've had you do my spot, but...so how much is the rent?"

"I'm charging her about fifteen hundred dollars a month."

"Fifteen hundred? Jeena, that's far more than what you paid, you little thief."

"I know that, Parri, but how am I supposed to save up for this business if I don't have the funds. Black is already taking care of all the bills, so this is on me. Besides that, he doesn't know I'm quitting my job yet."

"Really?" she answered in a very low and airy voice like she figured there was going to be some drama. She couldn't have been more wrong.

"I quit today. Well, in my mind I quit. I still have to call them and let them know."

"Without a two week notice?"

"Sure, why not? If they were to fire me, I highly doubt they would give me a writing in advance. That's why I am paying them the least with a phone call courtesy." I pulled into the parking lot of where I used to live. "Truth is, Parri. I don't want to go back to the place and work where I met Andre' at all. Everyone knows about what happened, and I could tell when I went back to work that people were talking about me behind my back. Things just weren't the same. Besides that, they knew of Andre' because he was treated there, and it felt plain embarrassing. I toughed it out, but now it's time for me to move on."

"I figured there was more to this whole quitting story besides it being for a change in career. You had to get away from a living hell, and if you feel that way," she said, opening her door wide, "then there's no sense in working in the fire."

"I agree."

When I stepped out of the car, all of the trauma came back and hit me in the heart. I hadn't been back to stay at my old spot overnight in such a long time, ever since the near death experience. I was living with Faith, my sister, who eventually sold her home to move out of town. I was thanking God that the people who bought her home weren't moving in until I got married, actually a good two weeks after, meaning the house was probably still vacant. That made it a comfortable stay for me while Faith moved out, and it kept me from living with and sleeping with my only other option – my then fiancé.

I could see Parri from the corner of my eye, picking me apart because she already sensed that I was slightly uncomfortable being in front of the condo. I glanced at the room window I wished I would have jumped from when Andre' attacked me the first time. The place brought back so many bad memories, but then, it also had very good times which was why I knew eventually, I would be able to come back to it.

"Are you sure you don't just want to sell it?"

"No." I shut my door, harder than what I wanted to shut it, causing it to slam. "Dang! Now I bet my window's off track." I opened the door back, but before I could fiddle with the glass, I noticed a woman walking up the path to the condo door.

She was tall, inches taller than me, but then again, I couldn't get an accurate detail of the height because of the heels she wore that were of spike design. I watched as she appeared to be on a mission, therefore, I only assumed it was the mission to meet me so I could give her the keys to her place as I took the deposit of first two month's partial payment. That way, I was always a month ahead with the payment just in case she decided to leave high and dry with no warning, stiffing me with the bill.

I glanced at the time on my cell phone. If it was the new tenant, she was early. Because of that, I continued to fiddle with my car window to make sure that it still worked post my door slam.

"Is that her?"

"I don't know if it's her or not, and no, I'm not sure if I want to sell it. Actually, my brain tells me it's better to make ongoing money off of it instead of a lump sum and keep it moving." My window seemed to be good, so I shut the door once again and tossed the keys in my bag. "What do you think?"

"Of your decision?" she asked.

"No. Her." I glanced over at the condo, forcing Parri to look that way as well. The assumed tenant stopped at the door – my door. It had to be her.

"The only thing you need to judge about her is her money. Anything else is irrelevant because as long as she can fix the crap she breaks and pay the rent on time while sticking to your rules, this should be a piece of cake."

At that, we walked up the concrete pathway until we got to our destination, and this was where we met the new tenant face to face. Just as I thought. She was tall in the heels, but she still appeared to be taller than me if she were to take them off. Her eyes were caked with makeup, but her face was foundation free. Other than that, she wore a navy blue skirt that came to her knees, and a white clutch remained intact between her side and arm. Did she look like she had money? Sure she did and lots of it, but looks could be deceiving. Even I was known to have an expensive appearance every so often when my closet was generally more toned down and casual.

"How are you? It's nice to meet you minus the internet and phone calls. I'm Jeena, and this is my best friend, Parri. Are you the new tenant?"

"I certainly am. I'm Lynia, and I can't wait to move in! It's been a while since I'm able to live on my own," she announced with a huge sigh. "So I'm all in."

"Really?" I glanced at Parri, and she immediately put her radar eyes up. "Why is that, if you don't mind me asking?" I unlocked the door, and into the empty space I walked with Lynia and Parri following closely behind.

"Bad and seriously long relationship, and now that it's over, I just want to start fresh in a bad ass condo. Yours fit the bill from what my friend said that met with you a while back, and you don't have to worry, I'm clean, alone and ready to take my life to a new level of happiness."

"Well that sounds great, Lynia."

"Seems like you two have a little in common," Parri blurted out, but then realized that her mouth went a little too far that time. The glare that I shot her burned through her bean head, and I wanted to slap each and every cosmetically whitened tooth from her mouth. Instead, I took a deep breath and played it off as Parri backed further away from my reach.

"In common? Were you in a pretty tough relationship?" Lynia asked, unaware of the awkward moment between Parri's words and my eyes.

I smiled, but I wanted to kick Parri's neck crooked, back out of the condo and change my mind about the whole move in my condo thing. The last thing I wanted was someone prying into my past love, likes or lusts that weren't so good. Being a married woman, the past, as bad or good as it was, had no business interfering with my present. I was so sick of it, but I put on a front and kept things friendly with the clueless tenant.

"Yes, actually. I was in a rough relationship, but now that it's over, I'm happily married and doing just great. That's why I know that you've made the right choice to move on and move in this condo alone and confident."

I should have gone into sales. I worked that line, and turned that negative into a positive. In the middle of it all, I was sweating like a bulldog in the desert, but other than that, it was time to kill the small and worthless talk to get to the talk worth something – my money.

After showing Lynia through the condo live and in person versus the photos sale we did, we sealed the deal. The contract was signed, and I left there with a month's worth of money to hold me over along with my savings until I got my interior design business off the ground.

"Sorry, Jee."

"Forget you, Parri." I turned the corner and forgot to shove her out of the passenger's side door. I prayed the Lord's forgiveness for the thought, but today, she was on my nerves so bad I could have fed her to the concrete. "Just what the heck is your problem? Do you make it a point to air my business to the world after I just told your loud mouth that I was uncomfortable with anyone finding out about me and what happened?"

"You must be," she paused, "mad?"

"Parri!" I pulled over to the side of the road. "This isn't funny. You're a hater."

"Say what?"

"A hater. Don't even think to tell me that what you said to the tenant about me having things in common with her was a slip of the tongue. What if I slipped and slapped the hell out of you? That would be a true slip." I gripped the stirring wheel, but didn't immediately press the gas. "You know what, Parri?" I asked as she sat there in my raggedy vehicle starring me in my mouth like I was saying something she couldn't believe. "You have a problem..."

"No, it looks like you do."

"What?" I couldn't believe she was turning it around on me in a failed attempt to throw me off of the subject. As I waited on her to retract her ignorant statement, she lifted her finger and pointed down the road to the light. My eyes followed, and there was Black. He wasn't at work, and he wasn't alone either.

Riding back home, I pretended that nothing was wrong when indeed, every single flipping thing in my brain had gone to chaos. After she'd notified me of Black in the car with a woman with her little, freshly manicured, pinky finger, I immediately shrugged it off as work related. What the heck else could it have been, right? There wasn't anything remotely cheater-ish about the whole thing nor Black...until Parri continued to dish more information, and my butt started eating it all up with a knife, spoon and fork.

"Here's the thing, Jeena. This really wasn't the first time I've seen him with that lady."

My eyes lit up like firecrackers in the night sky and got as big a round as bowling freaking balls. "Oh...what? You mean you know who is in that car with him from way back here?"

"Uhm hmm," she sang as she nodded her head while shutting her eyelids.

I watched Parri's head go up and down and then up and down some more until I took my hand off the wheel to slap her on the arm.

41

"Ouch! What was that for with your abusive ass?"

"Don't just sit there nodding, Parri! How did you just let me pass by Black without following him, and then you come out with some crap like that? What do you mean you saw him with her more than once? And how did you see them together? Shoot, when?"

"First of all, I don't know if it isn't strictly work related, so I allowed you to not get your panties all in a funky bundle and follow him frivolously because if you did, they would have spotted you, concocted a plan and if, and I mean if, he was doing something behind your back, they would have jumped to plan B, and re-strategized to start all over. Basically, they would have fooled you. Ain't your mom ever told you to not confront a man without full damn proof?" She took a deep breath after the long explanation, and then continued, "Secondly, I saw them together only three other times before you got married, but I couldn't find anything on him. Since you and him were ride or die, plus given the fact that he took a damn big ass bullet for you and your drama, I really didn't want to damage something that was potentially good since you were finally in real love and all." She flipped the visor down to look at her teeth. "There it is! I knew I felt a piece of that apple from earlier." She dug her fingernail in and flicked it out of the window.

This ho was crazy! She could talk about everything else straight up and down, but the stuff she really and truly needed to say, she kept silent. That was the dumbest, most insolent thing next to dogging Tanya's man out in front of her that Parri had done today – not tell me anything about Black before or after I married him. She was right though, as usual, about every single thing she said, and all I could do was huff and puff about crap I knew absolutely nothing about.

"Why are you looking at me?" she asked. "It was just an apple. Happens to everybody, Jee." As I continued to stare into what felt like her soul, she spoke again. "The road is that way, Jeena, and your house is right down the road. Green light, ma'am." Then, she noticed my eyes which were already tearing up tremendously. "Oh, Jeena!" she sang. "Pull over here, and get out."

I crossed the intersection and did exactly as she told me to do. I was about to be a total wreck, and my insides were about to look identical to the outside of my car – worthless. After pulling over, I got out of the car, and Parri was running so fast that she met me over on the driver's side before I could get two steps in.

"Hurry up. Go on," she rushed me in a tone that was more empathetic than what she'd sounded inside the car when she provided me the big reveal.

I got in the car, shut the door, and stared forward, imagining a huge, never ending tunnel with the words NEVER ENDING DRAMA painted on the walls in all caps. At that point, the first tear fell onto my skin, and I went into utter cry baby mode. I didn't even want to look at Parri because it seemed that I was always on the other end of her told you so's and bad news baring. In this situation, I didn't want to hear the word that I was repeating continuously in my mind – karma.

When I heard the gear shift, I watched Parri look at the side mirror until the traffic cleared to get back on the road. Before she saw me looking, I turned back to face my hands which were stagnantly on my lap. My wedding ring was in full showcase on my ring finger, and I slowly reached over with the fingers of my right hand to twist it from facing right side up. At that point, I didn't want to think about relationships – not Tanya's, not anyone's – not even my own. I was so shaken up over the thought of Black cheating on me that I literally wanted to be single...just for now. Single once again.

Parri was quiet on the short way back to my house. Never before had this happened, but I was feeling really envious of Parri's single life. I hated to admit it again, but despite her flaws, she had her head on straight. Thing was, I desperately didn't want her to be my voice of reason. Last year, it was both my sister Faith and Parri, in their own unique ways, telling me what I needed to hear. It took bullets and kicks to the ribs to turn me to God and into a better me. Unfortunately, it seemed like my change for the better was too late. Black could have possibly been cheating on me. That was my karma. I was about to become like Tina, the woman whose husband I sexed while she sat at home.

Parri finally pulled into my driveway as I continued to shove the tears from my cheeks, and then she leaned in with extra advice. "Jeena, everything is fine. It could be a work buddy, a friend, or even a damn cousin for all I know. The fact is that he is yours." She snatched my left hand up in the air. "I saw that shit." Parri turned my wedding ring right side up. "Don't you ever be ashamed of that. It's honorable, no dishonor in it. It's the cheating asses that are dishonorable. If he is cheating on you, digest it, but don't be ashamed. Be sad, but don't die."

Parri's words struck me like a knife to the heart. I felt like dying. I felt like crawling underneath a rock so that I wouldn't feel so dumb for talking to people about Black like he was the only good man on earth. If anyone knew about this...

"At this point, Jeena, he isn't cheating though. He was just riding. Are you sure you didn't recognize the lady either?"

Like hell I did. We made certain that we knew each other's friends, associates and the like before taking things to the level of marriage. We wanted openness, and it was Black's idea in the first place. There was to be nothing hidden which was what nearly got us killed in the first place. Secrets, in my case, ended up the root to all my evils, and it had to stop. The question that was eating away at me since Parri started talking about it was straight forward – was Black being truthful with me?

"I don't know her," I said quietly, dropping my head.

"Jeena," she replied, turning the car off. "It's fine. Just ask him about it if you want. Instead, just tell him you went for a ride and saw him crossing the intersection. See what he says. More than likely, he will mention everything, including about her being in the car. That way, it will put you at ease," she paused. "Jeena?"

I was contemplating passing out, but couldn't find the faintness I needed to do so. "Yeah?" I answered.

"It'll be fine. I never said he was cheating. It may be innocent."

Before I got out of the car, Parri grabbed my hand, and I wanted to take back every ill thing about her feeling jealous of Tanya and me because she didn't have a man of her own. When I thought about it, she probably was better off because when she let go of my hand, stepped out of my car and into hers to drive off, I didn't feel free anymore. Instead, I felt like I was in prison and needed to dig my way out.

As I stepped inside the house, I immediately began searching, digging, doing anything to find evidence of a cheating man. When I got to the second drawer, I just broke down. I didn't want to be this woman, not now and not ever. I just wanted to finally be in love and be bonded to that love inside someone else.

Lying on the floor crying, tears depositing onto my shirt, I tried to hold on to what I knew about Black for many years, even before we started dating. Then reality started to sink in as I stared around at the walls of my...our...bedroom. How many women did he have in this bed that I'd already made mine? How many different women walked naked in front of his mirror before or even after he started seeing me that he wasn't so up front about? Could I have fallen for a man who wanted to be married just so he could have his cake and more cake like Andre'? Could I have been duped?

My thoughts reverted back to the conversation I had with Black this morning after that colossal omelet I made for him, giving him most of it out of love. Any other man would have gotten nada, but he was my husband so I lived love a little. I remembered what he said to me – *"take a step back and play girlfriend some more. You know I like that."* Sure, what he said could have meant nothing, or for that matter it could have meant just what he said, he wanted me to play girlfriend. What if that was what he needed – a simple girlfriend.

I felt myself about to lose every strand of hair that I was born with from the root. I was now a wife. Was my sexy about to leave?

"This is the devil. Gotta be." Or either it was karma out to set the record straighter than I wanted it to be set. I needed my cell phone to call my sister. Running out into the living room, I dove onto the couch as if someone was aiming a pistol at me through the window, grabbed my phone, and dialed like a mad woman. She picked it up on the first ring.

"Faith," I stammered, "I need to talk to you. I'm about to break. I can feel it."

"Sis, well hold on now. Let me move from the table."

I listened to her excuse herself from what seemed to be company. It sounded like she was out and about early this morning brunching or something with someone. I hated to interrupt, but my physical, mental and spiritual well-being was about to go to the damned. I'd come too far to spiral out of control.

"Jeena, this sounds serious," she spoke into the phone as I heard her close a door. The echo through the phone alerted me to the fact that she was in a bathroom stall or something similarly as closed in. "Breathe and know that God is with you, even in the bad. All things work out for your good. Hold it together, and focus on only Him before you start to talk. Come on now."

"I don't even know what I'm really upset about, Faith. I'm feeling like I'm about to curse someone out and cry all at the same time. I'm just tired of it, Faith. I'm trying to live right and then here comes wrong again," I whined. Feeling like a child, I slid down from the couch and started to stare at my wedding photo. Then I raised my foot and kicked it off of the coffee table.

"What's going on?"

"I saw Black today, and he was supposed to be at work. I mean, I woke up, cooked for him, walked him outside, kissed and all that, but he ended up in the car with some woman!" I exclaimed, eyes bulged without a clue as to what was about to go wrong in my world.

"Do you know who the woman was?"

"No." I rolled my eyes because I knew good and well what was coming next.

"Did you find out?"

"No."

"Are you going to find out?"

I paused, but I guessed the pause was too long because Faith answered for me.

"Well, that's the first thing. You can't rightfully get angry if all you saw him with was a woman in a car. What were they doing in the car? Was that a relative? Was it a date? If it was a date, there's your problem. The bottom line is, at this stage or any stage in your marriage, riding around with the opposite sex is about to place trouble into the land of paradise and potential. Find out more to the story, but do it the right way. Remember, that you still have the ring and the upper hand with God. He won't leave you. If he's doing something wrong, God has your back, and He'll let you find out the full truth an easy way or a hard way, but it will be the truth setting you free to make a decision. Right now, this is premature guessing."

"It wasn't the first time he was with this lady according to Parri."

"Parri?"

"Yeah."

"How does she know?"

"She saw them together before we got married."

"Were they hugged up, kissing, looking awkwardly together but trying to hide it like grown-ups do when they're creeping?"

"I didn't ask. It was just the way she said it at first that got to me, but then she told me that she didn't bother about telling me because of all we went through. I assumed that when she said it that she didn't see anything major."

"So why is it bothering you so much? I've never been married, but I can tell you what they say. As soon as you marry, hell breaks loose on everything that you thought holds you to your man. It's that bond with God in the center that Satan hates, but know that he isn't strong enough to take anything from you, Jeena. God always wins, and you're on the winning side of the outcome every time, no matter what the odds are. Think about who is heading up your team."

"I know, but I just keep thinking about what I did in the past and what I deserve..."

"Stop it, Jee. You deserve just what God has for you, and whatever it is, because you have repented and love Him, you'll make it through it. Don't let your past start to chip away at your future, and, Jeena?

"What?" I slumped over, managing to look like Faith's child.

"Don't let people tell you about your marriage. The only person you should be talking to about that woman in the car is Black, and I'm positive that he has an explanation and your instincts will sort it all out. He loves you, big sis."

"Yes, ma'am," I responded jokingly.

"Bye. Call me later."

We hung up, and I felt stupid. Of course Black had an explanation for all of it, right? At least that was what I hoped.

I watched him as he hung up his clothes when he got home from work. My drink's ice had already melted, but I was faking the funk, pretending that the soda wasn't watered down when he would glance up into the mirror at my reflection while I stood at the bedroom door. I sipped whenever he looked up and gagged whenever he looked back down, preparing for his shower.

"Baby, what's wrong? You wanna get on this that bad? You like what you see?" he asked in a highly flirtatious way as he stood there, naked and sexy as ever. I wished I wanted him as much as he thought I did, but at that point, he was the last body I wanted to touch as I imagined him with another woman.

"No," I stated, but came back with a firm, yet fake, affirmation after a quick pause. "After you wash all those work germs off you and give me some of the smell I really like then I'll taste what's on you to see what's good." I couldn't smile, so I winked. Men saw winks as one way – horny, sexy, and a come on. A frown and a wink even equates to wanting nasty sex in their eyes.

"Oh, I smell too much like a flower for you, baby," he laughed. Little did he know, just in case he had a little bird on his arm chirping, nesting and pooping, I didn't want to lick up behind it.

"Speaking of work, how was it in your new position as manager?"

"Piece of cake. I knew the ropes before taking the position which is probably why they felt I earned the spot. Taking the initiative is what they called it. I call it keeping my lights on and food in my gut. God is good."

"All the time," I sang as my eyes followed him into the bathroom. When I heard the shower door slide shut, I sat that nasty drink on the dresser and headed over to the bathroom door. Then, I paused. His suit – he'd just hung it up in the closet. The old cliché was that if you look for something, you're bound to find it. Well, duh. That was the point of looking, so I didn't feel the least bit wrong about doing it. What would make me feel bad was if I didn't find one thing out of order in his coat, pants or underwear that had to do with a woman.

While he washed, I did the one thing I was going to hate. I searched. His closet wasn't the neatest in the land, but I knew exactly where to look, making the excavation that much easier. The pockets of his slacks were as dry as a bone, and when I fiddled around in his jacket, nothing turned up incriminating. Right after the closet search, there his cell phone sat, so there I went, right next to it on the bed.

There was nothing flashing on the screen, and that gave me a great deal of relief. As I unlocked it and poked until I got to the text messages, I was in such a panic that I swear I passed wind. If Black would've walked out of that bathroom or that shower turned off, I would've freakin' fainted to death. My heart was beating just that fast, but then it stopped...or at least I thought it did because I stopped breathing.

Text messages and there were lots of them. I saw text messages from a couple of days back to before we got married, even during our honeymoon. None of those text messages were to anyone I didn't already know, and most of those messages were short and sweet love notes to me. My paranoia tank sank, and I closed his phone out with the full lock, placing it back in the same spot on the bed.

"My sister was right. He loves me." I cradled the side of the bed by getting on my knees and asking the good Lord for forgiveness. It wasn't that I did something so bad, but it was just that I felt so bad about doing it. There Black was, loving me in the hardest way that he possibly could, and there I was with too much time on my hands. "Oh no!" I'd forgotten to call and quit my job.

I got up from the floor after finishing my prayers, got my cell phone and started to dial my place of last employment. When the operator answered, I just cut her off. She was one of the women who continued to spread the news about what happened between me and Andre', and every time I walked by, the word *slut* came like a laser from her eyes. I felt like I was in the twilight zone, and I was too ready to get away from the strange planet that I put myself on.

In cut off mode, I rushed, "I need to speak to Donna, please."

"Is this Jeena?" she sang to my ultimate gravity of disgust. My throat cringed and the vein in my head pulsated because I wanted to curse her out so bad, but the saved me wouldn't let my tongue go. I wasn't ever the turned up type of chick, but in this particular type of situation where I had to digest a hater in full force, I was ready to bash that skull.

"Yes," I swallowed, and as I stared up at the ceiling, I wanted my teeth to roll down my throat. Only God knew how hard being kind to her was for me. "This is Jeena."

"Well congratulations, girlfriend! It looks like you have gone and jumped that broom, huh? Everyone is talking about it, and we can't wait to see you. I already have your name changed in my books up here in the front, too. Jeena Black."

How the heck did they know my new last name...wait. The hospital and those HIPAA deregulated mugs. What good was the paperwork when healthcare providers pull all the records anyway to find out more juice and pass it along? Obviously, they got Stay Black's name from somebody knowing someone in the hospital where we were admitted, and the cat ran from there.

Forget her. "Donna, please?" I repeated abruptly.

"Okay then, well it sounds important, so let me transfer you."

"Tame my tongue today, Jesus, please, and I'm going to ask for forgiveness early if I mess up," I whispered during the call transfer.

Finally, I get Donna on the other end after listening to that horrific stall music that will force anyone to hang up the dang phone. "This is Donna," she answered with that nagging authoritative tone. I hated that with such a passion! Why on earth would someone want to sound like a stuffed nose and confuse it with professionalism?

"Hi, Donna, it's me, Jeena. How are you today?"

"Well hello, darling! Good to hear you're back because we have so much work for you to do when you come in. The new crew hasn't pulled their weight, so I will need you to train…"

Train?

"I quit." I hung the phone up in her face. She was one of the people happy to get the gossip and wouldn't stop it from going down. I faced the fact that I behaved like a whore only one year ago, but I wanted to change. Hanging up in her face was the best start to letting it all go. Now, it's time to tell Black because the shower stopped, and he would be exiting any minute.

Placing the words and thoughts that Parri gracefully tucked into my skull out of my mind, I re-entered the bedroom from the hallway, walked right up to Black and gave him a kiss on the lips – a no evidence found kiss on the lips.

"I like that, Jee." He backed up to get a better look at me while I enjoyed the look that I was getting at him.

"I have something to tell you, baby," I stated, putting my hand up to his lips to stop him from inquiring about it before I got started. Then, I ran my fingers through his wet dreadlocks, and continued, "I quit my job today." My fingers kept feeling through his hair, but my eyes concentrated on his naked shoulders. I couldn't look him in the eyes because I was a little uncomfortable already with how he may have reacted to my sole decision of leaving work.

"You quit? Why'd you quit, babe?" He asked, wiping his face again with one of the brand new hand towels that I bought specifically for the hands. Why he was using it for his face, I hadn't the slightest idea, but it perturbed me just a tiny bit. However, I didn't let it show. "Hey," he called me again, this time touching the bottom of my chin with his fingers, beckoning me to look back at his face.

To tell the truth, I didn't want him to find out just how much anguish I was going through at the job since the shooting and stabbing. I never told Stay Black that it was hell going back to work when I got well enough to return because everyone knew about what I did. Fact was that I didn't want to seem selfish for quitting, and a part of me also felt that I had to go through the trash talk behind my back, just deal with it, because I brought it on myself. That was my punishment to myself because for the longest I didn't forgive myself for Black nearly dying for me.

Anyway, I just felt I was grown enough to deal with the issues back then, but since we got hitched, I wanted to make a real new start. Sometimes people needed to start over, and that was what I wanted with my new marriage – a clean slate and new career – so I told Black only the good part of why I left, leaving the bad parts out.

"I want to go into interior design, starting with this place."

He laughed. "Is it still too late to get an annulment?"

"Black!"

"Just playin', baby," he reassured me, "I was just kidding. I already told you what you can do with this, but we're going to be looking for a new spot anyway, right? What do you plan on doing…using the money from your rental to get started because a brother's not making corporate money just yet."

"Exactly! See, I knew I wouldn't have to spell it out for you. I'm charging fifteen hundred dollars a month like I told you, and that's more than enough to contribute to the dreams I have and contribute to our savings."

"I'm not complaining, but I still want you to save most of your money while I pay the bills, Jeena. That's the only way we can get up outta here and rent this place out, too. We had a plan, babe. You're supposed to have about ten of my kids and all that while I sit back, watch television and you bring me my plate of ribs next to a cold..."

I shoved him in his chest, and he stumbled back like a basketball player in full flop mode. "We need to get an annulment right now if that's what you drugged me up to say and sign on our wedding day."

He looked to his left and right, and then ended up pointing to his dresser with a serious look on his face. "Check that drawer then. Contract signed, sealed and set. Go ahead."

"Are you serious? Stop playing, Black, because I know I didn't sign..."

"Come on over here. Stop stalling." He grabbed my hand and then I followed his damp body over to the dresser that I was searching through earlier. "Now, pull that drawer open for yourself."

It was the last drawer that I hadn't even had the chance to get to pry through, but obviously, if there was something incriminating in it, that drawer wouldn't have been it anyway because he was sending me straight to it. As I rolled my eyes and glanced back up at Black's handsomeness while he threw on a T-shirt and some baggy jeans, I leaned over to place my butt all in his face for a quick tease while he spanked it. Then, I pulled the drawer open to get the shock of my married life. Inside the drawer was a full out diamond tennis bracelet made just for me, the one that I showed him on our honeymoon! Needless to say, my vagina fell out, and Black got sweaty all over again. My tennis bracelet had a front row seat to...

My Joy.

After our huge love making session and my lovely gift, whatever Parri said... Wait, Parri who? She was my girl and all, but if there was anything I knew was that Black was in love with me. Another woman? Chile please.

We sat at our favorite restaurant in the city called Sleepless while I slid my feet outside of my sandals to massage the inner parts of his thighs. We were seated in an area of the restaurant surrounded by thin white, yet translucent, draperies that secluded our booth from the others. The moonlight shone directly on us, and even though that sucker was full and round, there were absolutely no signs of the mythological demon wolves or vampires out. Everything was going our way, the way newlyweds were supposed to have things go. I looked forward to them getting better.

"I thought I heard your voice!" squealed a woman as she peered her eyeballs through the draperies.

My eyes jolted open as if the woman may have been speaking to me for a moment, but then I watched intently as she paid absolutely no attention to me. Instead, her eyes were connected to my husband's, and he wasn't the least bit agitated at all. Her arm reached further inside the curtain, and because I didn't go with my gut that was telling me to pick up my fork and jab her in the arm, she was able to literally graze Black's go-tee with her fingers. My body went ham just like a pig, but I sat there with a stupid smile which was the Christian thing to do. Black, he didn't even look my way, but continued to speak, only pushing his head back ever so slightly as to not welcome the touch, or for more on point terminology - the fleshy fingers frolick, she just gave his jaw. I was losing my religion quickly while thoughts of banging her head into the corner of the table raced through my mind, and I needed a drink. Faith never told me that it would take all my being to not go off when I wanted to do it.

I just sat back and dissolved during the conversation until Black actually remembered I was sitting right there in front of them, both my feet tucked in the middle of his thighs. I wasn't about to move those bad boys either just in case Black lost his mind anymore than he already had. Someone would have lost a testicle. Truth was, the woman wasn't one of those crusty eye bimbo types. She was gorgeous, and I wasn't feeling that at all. My confidence level went to a negative slant, especially when she leaned my way and said...

"Hey, girl. You have a good man right here. I had no idea that my ex had gotten married to such a wonderful looking lady," she sang. "Well, you're going to love him. Take care." She looked over at Black. "We gotta get together some time me and you. Call me."

The hell? Call you sometime? Black needed to not ask me why I was looking at him like I was gonna jump over the table and snatch my wedding ring off his finger. Just who the hell was that, and why would she poke her head in and slob her hand all over your face in front of me and feel alright about it? Huh, Black?

Those words I thought, but my ears were the first to do anything. They listened to Black as he started in on the who, why and for what of the situation. He could sense that I was bothered at the least and about to throw my knife at the most, but with Black, nothing would ever get that bad because he had a great way of dealing with situations. Most of all, he had a special way of dealing with me.

"Jeena," he put his hands up in the air as he spoke, "Yo, baby, listen, that girl was wildin' out. Don't sweat that. I see right through that dumb smile on your face so you can go ahead and let the crap out. I don't deserve you to just about cuss me out, but I'll take it for not thinking fast enough," he laughed. "I was just as shocked as you were to have her reaching in on me like that, babe. My bad. That was an ex-girlfriend who pushes things too far, and that's what ended our relationship in the first place. Trust me, I had to let that chick down easily because everything is extra with her." He stopped and then looked up. "Imagine my face when she planted a kiss on another man's lips in front of me when we were together, just to make me jealous after not agreeing with her earlier that day. What I'm saying is, you can get mad, but she ain't nothing to get mad at. The chick's crazier than what she seems. She's nothing impressive, believe that."

I kept my cool, and my anger dwindled when Black put it that way. Besides that, I was his wife, ring and all, and she had nothing on that. Black had always made sure I had that lock and key, even when my confidence hit the downward slope for a slight moment. Still, I hoped to God I never saw that karma stricken female again or any of his ex's for that matter. The bad thing was that ever since she left the table, that gut feeling of doom came back, like my past was going to come back and bite me – hard! Sushi was what I ordered while Black ordered some great looking shrimp dish that set my taste buds off when I sampled it, so we finally started chomping down.

"You better move back, Jee," he stated, hovering over his plate to protect it from my paws. "Long eyed...you had a menu just like me. You could've just gone down to the beach and caught that fish you're eating. Now this shrimp...you couldn't hook it if you tried."

"Oh shut up, Black. Just give me another taste," I begged, and he obliged by allowing me to take it from his fingers.

It melted in my mouth, and then I leaned over the table and gave him a big kiss, we finished eating and left Sleepless.

We forgot to leave any lights on at the house, so it was pitch black once we got there. Black ended up planting so many bushes in the yard near the porch that it looked like a darkness overflow at night. I couldn't even see the porch at all because he didn't clip the bushes all week due to the honeymoon.

Before getting out of the car, Black grabbed my hand. "I love you. I was thinking about what happened back at Sleepless. If I offended you by kidding about my ex, I'm sorry. It wasn't a joke, and I've been on the other end of that before, so..."

"No, I'm good, baby. It shook me that much," I responded by lifting my fingers and throwing up a pinch sign.

"So we're good?"

I smiled. "Yeah, always."

At that, he exited the car, but this time, I didn't wait for him to come open the door for me. As I cracked the door open myself, my heart dropped to the pavement, bounced back and slapped me back in the mouth so hard that I couldn't even speak. Black was on his way to the passenger's side so I shut the door back quickly and remained stationary in the car, staring down at the stick...

The pregnancy stick.

"What the hell was it doing there, Parri?"

"I don't know, with your dumb ass. I didn't put it there, and that's for damn sure," she said, tossing what sounded like a cracker in her mouth. "You should have stopped his ass in his tracks and then shoved that urine soaked sucker right in his face." She paused as I waited to hear an answer, any answer, that would put me at ease. "Tell you the truth, I don't know what the hell is wrong with you."

"Me?"

"Yeah. Wake up, and stop acting like you're not here. If you find a pregnancy test in your man's car that isn't yours, that alone gives you a license to slap the teeth out of his mouth unless that shit belongs to his sister or mom. To top it off, Jeena, you just got back from your honeymoon!"

It was happening all but too soon. Karma came, and she wasn't going anywhere fast. Tears began to well up in my eyes while I heard Parri's crunching. Then, I started to think about what Tanya's mom told her about men, that they all cheat, the good ones and the bad ones. Then, I thought about myself. They cheat with women like me. I hung the phone up in Parri's face, and seconds later, it vibrated some more. I didn't answer it. I was a wreck, and Black was in the bed sleeping as I sat on the toilet weeping. The clock on the cell phone read three a.m. through my blurry eyes, and as I wiped, I came to grips with what I was going to do. I was gonna go get that pregnancy test out of the car.

Breathe, Jeena, breathe and stay calm. I opened the bathroom door, and peered down the hallway. Then carefully, I started to disable the alarm system but decided not to because the numbers on the dial were so loud when pressed, and when disabled, a man's flippin' voice would come on the recorder and say "*system disarmed*". That would in no way be cute because the first thing I could see is Black waking up and questioning me about where I was going this early in the morning. Shoot, I would look like the dang cheater!

Only the doors and a couple of windows were armed, so I made it my task to open the bedroom window across from our bedroom because that one had no trigger on it. On top of that, it happened to be the closest in feet to the car in the driveway.

"Crap! The stupid keys." I launched myself into the bedroom as quietly as possible and grabbed my bag while Black was still sound asleep. Then, I crept back into the neighboring bedroom again, leaving a crack in the door as I walked back toward the window.

Again, it was pitch black outside, and lucky me, I didn't think to turn on the outside night light before coming out. I wasn't about to turn back around and run down the hall to do it either. With my luck I would trip, fall, and end the fiasco by waking up Black.

My right foot led the way outside after I tossed my keys over in the dirt near the car. The dang things were shaking too much, so I had to get rid of them. Tossing them was the option I chose. Then I grabbed the window sill tightly so I wouldn't fall head first directly into the sticky bushes that Black planted right up on the house to prevent breaking and entering crap like this. As I eased my left foot out of the window, the first thing I did was look both ways down the road to make sure there were no cops driving by because that would be hell in a dang hand basket. I didn't want to be handcuffed in my pajamas standing outside my own house.

Scurrying over to the car, I picked my keys up from the ground and rushed to the passenger's side of the car. Upon opening the door, as soon as I stepped backward, my foot landed right on something sharper than swords that penetrated my foot.

"Ouch!" I yelped, landing atop the door so that it would hold me up from landing on the ground. "Dang it, slip shine, shiiiiii....Jesus, help me, dear Lord," I continued while I maneuvered myself into the seat. After dropping in the dead center of the seat, the pregnancy stick came directly into my view. My heart started to race, and I glanced back at the window and then back behind myself at the road. Then, I picked it up, re-thought that idea, and then, tossed it back down.

"I need a glove or a tissue." At that, I started searching Black's immaculately clean interior for a piece of old paper or something that I could carry the piss stick with. "Forget it." I couldn't find a thing, so I toughed it out, urine or no urine.

When I picked it up, the results were flipped upside down, so I took a deep breath and turned the stick over. When I got the results, I just shut the car door and stared down at it like it was an untruth. I wanted the sky to fall right on top of me so the clouds could come and take me up, up and away because the pregnancy test read positive, and this dip stick isn't even mine.

I closed my eyes and dropped the stick on the passenger's side floor board, and the tears began to run. This wasn't how my marriage was supposed to start off. There was some chick actually doing the same thing to my man that I did with someone else's, except this one got me in the worst way. Black got someone pregnant. Had to be, unless he had a vagina he wasn't telling me about somewhere hidden next to his butthole and his back with a uterus and a growing womb.

The longer I sat in the car, the more I boiled over with rage, my eyes completely shut as I thought about the woman who I saw earlier driving along with Black, probably giggling her butt off while Black planned his next move with me. But just like Tina said before she stabbed me in my chest, all men slip up. This was Black's slip up, but I felt like I'd gotten stabbed over and over again emotionally in my heart.

Just as I reached the latch to open the door after retrieving the stick, my eyes popped open as I felt the door being blocked, hitting something that I had no idea was there. It was Black, and he was gawking, though dazed and confused, right at me and that pregnancy test in my hand.

This mo' foe better not act like he didn't know. Black didn't move, so I shoved the car door as hard as I could to knock his leg back. Although I hit him hard, I didn't feel better, and that was when Parri's words came full force about slapping the hell out of a man after finding a pregnancy test. That was when I pushed myself out of the car, pregnancy test in hand, slammed the door and then knocked his face the hell out with my palm.

"Jeena!" Black yelled, "What the hell you hit me for?"

"What the hell did I hit you for? You messin' around on me, that's what! Work? Was that where you were? At work?"

"Yeah, Jee. At work!" All Black had on were his boxers and socks, so it was apparent that he wasn't prepared for anything, especially that slap. Honestly, I wasn't ready for it either. When I hit him, I stalled like I'd committed the worst travesty on earth, but it sure felt good to smack the heck out of him for having a positive pregnancy test in his car that didn't belong to me – Mrs. Black.

"Well who was the heffa riding around with you in the car today, huh?" I asked, leaning myself back like I was at the wheel, dropping swag and money on a broad.

"What?"

What was all he had to say? Typical, right?

"Black, do you think I'm stupid? Look at this!" I held the stick close enough to his face that the tip grazed his nose, and he knocked it from my hand, causing it to land in the dirt. "Now, who the hell did you knock up because it certainly wasn't me!"

To my surprise, Black didn't answer. All he did was stare at me as I yelped like a monkey with a high pitched voice in the driveway. The neighbor's outside light came on, and Black looked up immediately. Then, he retreated into the house without saying another word to me, his hands up in the air like he was completely done. To add to the insult of the pregnancy test, he slammed the door shut behind him. When I yanked the test off the ground, I also heard him shut the bedroom window that I climbed out. The last thing I heard was a window lock.

I ran over to the window, and yep, through the cracked blind, I watched him walk back into our bedroom and slam the door. When I attempted to lift the window back open, a filthy roach crawled across my fingernail and I reared back, slipped and fell right into the sticker bushes. The thorns hurt me so bad on my legs until I rolled into one big flip to the side, landing my knees on the pavement.

Despite the pain I was in and the neighbor who'd had just opened up his door, I ran to my front door and started banging, promising myself that I would put my house keys on the car key ring as soon as possible so nothing like this would happen again. When Black didn't come to the door to let me back into the house, I started ringing the doorbell violently until I finally turned the knob. The crap opened, and as I closed it back after entering, my eyes caught Mr. Coach in his red slippers watching my antics from the side of his yard. I totally unraveled.

"Mind your freakin' business." I slammed the door my hardest, turned around and faced my worst fears. My marriage was no longer perfect, so I fell down on my knees, cried and prayed, with the pregnancy test right beside me...

On The Bare Floor.

That was where I woke up, all alone, and next to that pregnancy stick, not the man with whom I was so in love. My mind was in a fog, and my mouth a big wreck. Black...I didn't even know if he was gone to work or still in the bedroom, so I got up to check. Whatever time it was, I didn't know, but by the looks of the blinds, there was no sun up in the sky yet.

Before going into the bedroom, I stopped at the bathroom in the hall. My eyes were big, huge sacks of bags and cotton puffs from all the weeping I did over myself and my marriage, for hitting Black and for... Wait? Why was I the one so guilt ridden? By his not answering me, I knew for a fact that he was creeping, had crept, and probably sneaked up out of the house before daylight hit just so he wouldn't have to play the defense.

Placing the pregnancy test on the counter after wrapping it up in globs of tissue and washing my hands down in the hottest soap and water possible, I finally left the bathroom to enter the bedroom. Black wasn't there. When I walked across the room into the bedroom's bathroom, he wasn't in their either, therefore, I backtracked.

Everywhere was empty of Black, underneath the bed, in the closet, the kitchen, backyard, and even the extra bedroom. He was gone. I ran back to his closet and counted the suits because I knew how many he had, and one was missing. Then, I ran to check his underwear drawer, and they were all there, meaning that he didn't leave me for good. All I could do was drop onto the bed and sulk until I got the best idea I'd had since the smack down outside. I called Faith in the wee hours of the morning.

Her phone rang and rang until the answering machine picked up, so I hung it up and tried again, hoping I wouldn't get that greeting that she recorded of herself singing horribly into the receiver anymore. On what I thought was the last ring, Faith finally picked up and my head went underneath the covers. I was in desperate need of repair.

"Jee-eena," she groaned, but I didn't have time for that moaning. I knew she didn't have time for me either so early in the morning. It didn't matter because I needed her again, just like I did last year, but this time it was my marriage that was busting up.

"Faith, I need you to get up. Please get up because I don't know what to do now." My voice was quivering, so I knew the next stop was her flipping out to find out what was the matter. I removed myself from underneath the covers and sat up on the bed, clinging to the sheets.

"Jeena, what's wrong? Are you okay? What's the matter? I need to come down?"

Her questions continued over my breathing, and as the sound of her voice escalated and the questions continued to pour, I stopped her with an answer. "Black...he's cheating on me."

It sounded like Faith dropped the phone as the silence rushed in, concealing my breathing. As I waited on her response to the atomic bombshell I just let drop in the middle of my bedroom, I gathered a visual of the emptiness of the room that reflected the emptiness I felt in my life. That was when hopelessness crept in, beginning to cradle me as I sat atop my bed.

"No he's not, Jeena," she responded in disbelief, but I quickly corrected her, understanding that all she had to go on about Black was the great character in which I painted him...but without the newly discovered pregnancy test.

"No, Faith, he is. I found a woman's pregnancy test in his car. I told you he had a female riding in his car earlier, and I brushed it off. We went out to eat and bam, it was there, big as day as I got out of the car."

"I'm so sorry, Jeena. What did he say about it?"

"What could he say, Faith? After I hit him in his face, he didn't even speak to me." I dropped my head into the pillow. "He's not even here right now. He's probably with her concocting a strong defense against me, his own wife."

"He didn't say anything?" she asked in utter shock. Then she moved her thoughts to the pregnancy test. "Was it positive or negative?"

"Positive. The thing," I stated in the purest form of disgust known to mankind, "read positive."

"Just calm down, sis." Faith let out a deep breath, and I could tell that stuff just got real on her end of the phone. "Let's pray because it's easy to lose control in a situation like this, I'm sure. You already knocked him in his face, and he's already gone. Did he move out of his own house, or did he just leave for the night?"

I closed my eyes tightly as the worst migraine began to make the veins in my head thump so hard I thought one would pop at any second. Placing my cell phone on speaker, I laid on my back and held my head with the palms of my hands while my cell phone laid across my chest on speaker phone.

"He left for the night I assume, but hey, what else is to be expected, Faith? He got busted."

"You still have to hear his side, Jee. It looks obvious, I mean it really looks like he was having an affair and knocked someone up, but do you even believe that it's not that cut and dry after this man took a bullet for you? I mean, I see the way he adores you, sis. Not to knock what you're saying, but before I left, I felt comfortable leaving because I was convinced he had your back over everyone else. Girl, I just don't want this to be true, but I have your back one hundred percent."

"You think I jumped the gun, don't you?" I weeped. "If you would have seen the look on his face after I hit him, Faith. He just didn't respond like a man who'd been caught, but more like a man who was disappointed, not in himself, but in me."

"Wait a minute, don't go beating yourself up. At the same time, you let your instinct to attack take over..."

"Because of Parri."

"Parri?"

"Yeah."

"Huh?"

"She told me to smack him indirectly. It was in my head already, so I did it. It made sense, Faith, and it matched my mood at the time."

"She already knows?"

"Yeah."

"Why didn't you call me first, Jeena? You don't go calling people who escalate things. Not to talk about your friend, but you're in a marriage," she stressed. "You can't just jump the gun."

She paused. "Do you need me to come down there again? I can, just let me get my clothes on, and I'll be there in an hour."

Because Faith no longer lived close by, I hardly ever saw her except for on Sundays in church. Except for that, we talk on the phone much more to make up for the absence of seeing each other all the time. I wasn't going to lie, I needed someone to lean on, and Faith was the one who wouldn't only tell me the truth about a bad situation. She would do so in a way that wouldn't escalate it, such as giving me a viewpoint diverting around the slap to the face, in other words. Parri went straight for the jugular and slice. Always turned up. Death to follow.

"No, Faith, don't come. You were there for me when I had no sense at all, but now, it's time for me to become the older sister that I need to be. You can't always come to my rescue. I'll handle it...get to the bottom of it when Black comes back home. Just pray for me, sis, because this ain't right."

"Okay," she sighed, "I'll be here. Phone on."

"Love you."

"Love you, too."

"I don't know how the test got in my car, Jeena!"

I'd been up waiting on him for three whole hours, legs crossed Yoga style, rocking back and forth like I belong in the insane asylum. The pregnancy test sat atop his dresser all wrapped up like a swaddled infant, and when Black came in and saw it, he knocked it off his dresser in a rage. Maybe that wasn't the best idea of a greeting, but what else do you give a man who stays out before work in the early hours of the morning?

During his whole exit from the house, which I missed, it looked like he'd forgotten his cellular phone. What a bummer because he had to return to the house which killed his diss Jeena high. I had no idea that he left his phone in here, and that was messed up because if I would've known, I would have pounced on those recent calls.

He thought he was slick, claiming the *I'd never cheat* lie that every man on earth stuck to until death do them part. That wasn't to be used on me. Any man with a pregnancy test knew how it got there, whether they were willing to say was another.

"Black," I spoke, and he punched the top of the dresser with his fist. Whatever. That didn't phase me one bit. It was his fist, not mine, that would need a wrap when he's done.

"I said I don't know!"

"Why won't you just tell me? I saw you with a woman in your car yesterday. Is it hers?"

Black stared at me again with that look that even confused me. It was quite awkward, but I wasn't going to let it replace his answer to my question which I failed to ask directly with the straight up question of *who did you knock up?*

"You say it like I was with a woman yesterday, Jeena? I wasn't *with* a woman. That woman was a woman who owns the company I work for, Jeena. She comes in periodically and has lunch with those who work for her. It's a small, close knit company, so she's hands on. That's part of the reason I got the management job, Jee."

"Answer the question, Black."

"I just did and for the last time!" Black was about to snap, and I could tell that I'd pushed him to his limit with accusations apart from proof. Did that stop me? Nope. I knew good and well that anger was an attempt to shield, and I wasn't buying his story with all the money in my bank account. I would have bought a divorce first.

"The woman I saw you with looked your age or younger, so an owner of the company, I'm not buying, Black. No owner looks like..."

"Beautiful, Jeena? Yeah, she's our age, and she's not some old woman either. She's extremely gorgeous," he stressed, popping up and down on his tip toes. "Is that what you wanted? What about this? She's the heir to the company, Jee. Her father left it to her two years ago, and instead of putting us out of work by closing it, she used her good heart and let us work and move up, working on expansions." Before I could interject, he continued, "And oh yeah, she's single as hell, too!" he said clinching his fists with a huge smile on his face. "She's been single since me and you got together, and I don't know if she's pregnant or not." Black suddenly calmed down all his shenanigans and stared straight at me. "All I can tell you is that if she is, it isn't mine because I never slept with her because I'm in love with you. Top that off with the fact that she never tried to sleep with me in the first place, that should cover it."

I sat there on the bed, still in my Yoga position, trying to find a way to take my foot out of my mouth. Unfortunately, there wasn't any way to grab it and remove the dang thing. I wasn't gonna go out like that though, even though it sounded like every word he spoke was the absolute truth. As I sat on the bed, Black's rage softened as he approached me about what he saw as false accusations.

"Jeena, I would never cheat on you," he started as softly as he could. I could tell it was almost hurting him to speak in the tone he chose, but he continued and I listened. "But let's make this thing clear, if I did get someone pregnant, sure, I can take a couple of slaps because I would've deserved it. Since I didn't get anyone pregnant nor did I cheat on you since I've been with you, don't you ever put your hands on me like that again. If I do give you good reason, I'll tell you to slap the hell out of me myself. Thing is, Jeena, I'm innocent, and if I did something like that, I wouldn't defend it."

I just stared at him with no excuse for how I'd possibly jumped the gun. Still, no matter what he said, I didn't fully believe him. I would have been a fool to believe him, so I asked," So am I supposed to believe that she, or somebody, just dropped it in your car?"

"Believe what you want to believe. All I'm saying is that we just got married, and I'm trying to love you in every way that I can. I'm not going to lie and say I don't understand why you are upset. If I found a condom in your car, I would hit the roof, too, but I'm asking you to believe me and let this go. When I tell you that I don't know how that thing got in my car, I don't." He paused before he started to speak again. "I've never lied to you before, Jeena, and I won't start."

I could've broken a brick because I was so mad, and at that point, I knew the one thing I never thought would be tested was being tested – our trust in each other. As I watched him remove himself from my presence after straining himself to give me a kiss on his cheek, I forced myself up from the bed and walked quickly to catch up to him before he opened the front door. It was time for him to go to work for real this time, and I wanted to show that I was still claiming this marriage to him even in this rocky time. That was why I grabbed his hand at the door, even though I felt a load of tension in between us, and kissed him on his lips. He kissed me back, looked me in my eyes while remaining speechless, and left. I shut the door. We were in our first stages of ...

<u>Marriage Turmoil.</u>

I drove. It was something I did when I needed to run for cover, and that was obviously Black's way of dealing with issues as well. This time, cover was Tanya. Parri steered me wrong-ish already while Tanya couldn't steer, so all I needed from her was a bit of ventilation and breeze. It was always more peaceful to sit in someone else's nonsense versus your own at times, and I knew that wasn't the right thing to think, but I did. It worked. Many times, once examining the crap others go through, your crap doesn't seem half as dire, thus, to Tanya's crap I went.

Besides all that, Tanya was accustomed to getting dogged out by men. Not that I was absolutely certain that I knew what was going on with my husband after listening to his excuse that revealed nothing, but if I was to gain inspiration from a real life horror story, it would be Tanya. She'd survived it all, and now, she was working on marrying the madness. That was some forgiveness in action, not in just words. Faith could say it and do it, but she wasn't in a relationship. Parri simply wasn't about that relationship drama life, but Tanya, she was more a real life, been there done that model for me to at least examine.

It was nine o'clock in the morning, so Tanya should have been at home, but when I got there, she wasn't. Instead, it was Tony the trippin' who answered, and I took two steps back from the door when he spoke. Weed was the smell that he gave me, so I knew full well the children were gone because Tanya didn't play that...at least I thought.

"She's not here, Jeena."

"Oh yeah, I can tell that." I watched as the smoke drifted from his nostrils, making a failed attempt to seep into my shirt. "Tell her I stopped by."

"I sure will, Jee. You wanna come in and wait on her. She should be back in a couple hours."

Did he just ask me to come inside while Tanya was outside for a couple of hours? My mind went karate all over his weeded brain, but my body stood there in a stupefied condition as he continued to undress me with is red and crusted eyeballs.

"You know you're that type of female. Don't act like you're too good to do it now that you're saved and all."

Tanya told him my business! After all I went through protecting her from him, she really told this mug my bad business! Even worse, that joker was standing up in front of me serious as Satan was when he tempted Eve. The newsflash was that I wasn't Eve – anymore. I wouldn't cheat on Black or my friendship with Tanya if he was the last freaky man on the planet Earth.

I kept my position on the cracked cement beneath my feet, folded my arms and refused to allow that slobber mouthed mut to get underneath my skin. He hadn't changed one bit, but obviously fooled Tanya into marrying him. Bingo! Parri was dead on once again! I was such a bad judge of continued character, always giving things and people the benefit of a doubt.

"Yeah, I'm saved now, so I guess that prevents me from telling you what I would have said when I wasn't living so well which is eff you. So glad I'm living for the Lord now, so I'll just tell you to get a life because the one you're living now is full of ish, if you get what I'm trying to say in my unique kinda special way?"

"You won't be Tanya's matron of honor long, baby girl, if you tell her about this and how you tried to sleep with me over here," he lied. "She won't believe shit you say over me. Besides that, her phone is off, so I'll get to her first. If you don't come in, you lose a friend, Jee baby." He took another puff of that weed, and as he puffed, I dialed. While I dialed, I smiled back at him flirtatiously, and not surprisingly, his dumb butt smiled back.

"Hello, I believe someone is harassing me and smoking weed by the name of Tony. I'm at the address of 1530 Berrywild..."

"Shit, shit!" Tony dropped his weed, stomped it to a disaster, jumped from the door frame that he was leaning on, and snatched my phone from my hand, hanging it up before I finished the complaint to the cops.

"Gimme my phone!" I screamed, snatching it back, and the squeal of my voice caused him to clam up and freeze like the cops were right there.

"See you trippin'! Leave, go!" he yelled, backing back into the apartment while I gave myself two points and a pat. Anyone could look at him and tell he was on probation or had warrants, so why he decided to try me like that was ignorance on his part. I enjoyed watching his tired, saggy mouthed and saggy pants butt sweat, and I couldn't wait to tell Tanya.

"And he came on to me!"

"That's an ignorant mug for her to marry, now isn't it? And don't you go and tell her one thing about his screw up either."

"Why not, Parri?" I asked, sipping on a soda I scooped up from the drive thru of a fast food joint. I was so tired that I needed caffeine from anywhere to keep me awake on the road. I still hadn't told Parri about the encounter with Black over the pregnancy test, and I was happy she hadn't asked about it yet.

"Because if he didn't teach her that playing with fire kills the first time, then she needs to learn that crap the hard way. She went off on me for telling her the damn truth, so let her marry his ass. When anybody gets plenty warnings before marrying the person they are going to marry, the last thing a person wants to do is forget all the warning signs and get hitched anyway. Forgive it maybe, but don't make a damn lifelong decision on forgetting the crap."

"I have to tell her because that wouldn't be right, Parri. It puts me in the middle of it, and that's where I don't want to be."

"Well, I'm at work, so I'm out. Call me later and tell me about you and your man with his pregnancy test. I gotta go. You better call me too, or I'm coming to your house to dish it to him. You know I'm a jealous ass...or so you say."

She hung up in my face with the slam of a lifetime. I knew what she was waiting on. She wanted to put mud all over my face with another I told you so, but I wasn't going to let her. This time, I was really hoping that she was wrong about the insinuation of Black being with another woman, no matter how I felt. Even if he was sleeping around on me, it was time to prove Parri wrong, even if she was right. Her head was too swollen, and it was time for it to bust.

"Come on, baby, be telling me the truth," I said to myself as I pulled up to a hot fast food spot so that I could get Black some spicy wings and salad for lunch with a huge burger on the side. Some of the wings would be for me, and of course I would mangle a portion of this colossal salad. All in all, I wanted me and Black back, the way things were before the pregnancy test and the woman in the car. Why did things have to be so complicated? Whatever happened to easy love?

The floral shop that Black managed was fairly big, although a small company, if that made any sense. It was actually bigger than most floral shops that I'd been familiar with in the past. The small amount of shops like this that I'd been in only had a couple of employees as well as a seriously small collection of flowers. Black's shop had about fifteen employees, and everyone had something to do. New flowers came in every single week, and it was the job of a selected employee to not only learn about the plant but take care of particular plant families as well. Black taught me about the whole set up, including the wheel of water they freshen the plants up with, which explained the shop's former name Wheel of Flowers. Everything done there worked on a three hundred sixty degree rotation for the plants each day, inspecting them and more, which is why people paid an arm and a leg for a great bouquet that came with the accessories that keep them alive. People paid a good penny for their flowers, but there were also wonderful specials for most people to share in the exquisiteness of it all.

Pulling up to the newly named Garden of Eden, I braced myself for the worse response from Black, but I prayed for a response that could get us back on track – starting with the lunch date. Grabbing the bag of food from the car, I checked my outfit before going inside. I wasn't the best dressed or best looking wife to set eyes on, however, I'd had a long night. Make-up did wonders for the travesty I dragged out of the house. I was also certain that Black needed as much down time as he could get as well, so regardless of suspicions, I wanted to at least start off by breaking the ice between us that was thickening despite the kiss we left off with at the house.

The sun felt like it was roasting my back that was fully exposed in a backless tank while my jeans felt like they had roots growing from my thighs. It was going to be a terribly hot day, and as I opened the doors to the shop, the cool air hit me like an ocean wave. The smell was so alive and absolutely breath-taking that any measure of anxiety was relieved as soon as I walked inside. Just like the Garden of Eden, it was where we were supposed to be...

Until Adam and Eve Showed Out.

There they were, and I nearly dropped the food on the shop's wax washed floors. I didn't even have to place my feet ten steps inside before I saw Black and that dang woman that he was riding with in the car! The both of them were inside the doorway that read over the top EMPLOYEES ONLY, but to me, it didn't feel like they were anything employee like. Sure, I knew for certain that they worked together, however, that made me feel even worse because he could've potentially been with her more than he was with me! What happened to the periodic get together? This was two days in a full dang row!

I started to back up out of the shop one foot at a time, keeping my head down with a faked confused expression on my face like I'd forgotten something inside the car. I didn't want to bring too much attention to myself at all, but that failed when I bumped into an employee on the way out.

"Oh, excuse me! I'm so sorry, Mrs. Black."

And the person just had to know my name.

"Oh no no, don't worry about it. I just forgot something in the car, and I have an emergency back at home. If you would give this to Mr. Black for me? I have to run, and..." I just took off. I had to do it. I simply shoved the bag into her hand, about faced and left. So much for my Garden of Eden experience.

"But I'm sure Mr. Black would want to see you. He's right..."

Talk to my hot, sweaty back, I thought. Was it an overreaction? Maybe, but it was my overreaction, and I preferred, at that moment, to not see him with any woman at all, not even his mother, after the trauma of a pregnancy test in his car. Getting to my car never looked so good – the piece of wreckage.

Slowly but surely, I felt myself criticizing everything in my path, from the windshield wipers to the dusty air, the misspellings on signage to the way people walked down the street. The reason for the critical behavior was all on me because I failed. I failed to complete marriage mission number one because I didn't want egg on my face at Black's workplace. How hideous would that have been in front of another woman? No...in the face of a potential other woman, I wanted to remain calm, cool and...my phone rang.

"Hello?"

"Jeena?"

"Yes, who's speaking?" I asked, turning into the intersection.

"This is Lynia, the new tenant. How are you?"

Surprised to hear from her, I responded, "Well, I'm fine. How are you? Are things going well so far?"

"Yeah, sure, everything is great! I'm loving the place except, I think I'm missing a key."

"Missing a key? I didn't give you all the...oh!" I suddenly remembered that the patio door had a storage space that locked. The good thing was that it was still on my key ring. "The patio right? I'm so sorry, Lynia."

"No, I know. It was an honest mistake. I was just trying to pack things in when I noticed that one key didn't fit all."

"It sure doesn't. Again, my bad. I can swing over right now to drop it off if you like. It's no problem. I'll be right there if you're waiting."

"I sure am. Thanks, Jeena."

"Sure thing." I hung up. "I can't believe I did that." I stared into my rear view to make sure there was no sign of Black following me, although, I did hope that would happen to make it sort of a rescue the damsel type deal. It didn't happen, so on I went to my old spot. I hoped the chick I gave the food to told Black I dropped it off and didn't eat it herself. That would be just my luck.

Pulling up to my previous address, I was left with what ifs. What if me and Black didn't work out in marriage? What if the marriage was a whole load of back up sex hoopla, and since the tango and bango, there was nothing left? What if I accidentally gave Black the hero complex while at the same time he was my rebound guy? And last but not least, did we get together in marriage because of our willingness to ride or die for each other? Maybe I was over-thinking our love for each other, creating the second and third guesses, but I couldn't help it. Emotions were known to do just as much harm than good, and I found that out first hand. Either way, I was married, and it was really until death do us...

"Hi!"

I'd barely got my foot on stable ground in front of the door before she opened sesame. Way too bubbly for my taste Lynia was, but her money was just right. That made her much more tolerable.

"Hi there," I stated with a plastic smile. I wasn't in the mood for the champagne and celebration she looked like she had going on in the condo all by herself. The music was up and just over complaint range while I sniffed the smell of...

"Come on inside for a sec. Take a load off and try some of my steak and salad." She tossed a piece in her mouth. "I need the company, and it's delicious!" She slopped and licked the juice from the marinade from off her lips. "This steak is so good, I'm drooling. Got time?"

I thought why not? I needed a steak and a drink after passing on lunch with my husband, basically delivering him to the so called owner of the joint. A bomb ready to blow I was, but I couldn't allow the anxiety from my marriage to show. Besides that, I still had to tell Tanya about her man later, so it looked like my life was getting worse by the moment. There it went – my cell phone.

"Sure, I'll come in and chow down on a steak. Lemme get my phone really quick." Lynia left the door open and skipped her happy camperness back toward the kitchen while I looked at the ID. It was Black. "Hello?"

"Why did you drop all this good food off and then leave, babe? I was in the back, and I know you didn't think I could eat all this alone. What emergency did you have?"

"I had to come and deliver a key to the new tenant," I said, stepping away from the door while breathing a sigh of relief for thinking fast on my feet, knowing my true reason for dodging the flower shop had nothing to do with the tenant.

"I thought you already took care of that?"

"Yeah, I did, but I forgot one, so I'm over here now so..." I went silent for about two seconds, and he caught it. He was a dang me pro.

"Yo, Jee, look, baby. We can get through this. You have to trust me. I was thinking about it all night, and then I came in here to work, but look...let's just squash it. I promise you, I've never cheated on you. Not ever. I can't prove it though, Jee. Please, baby, let's not do this. I love you."

The problem with what Black said was that I honestly knew how easy it was to put on a front and tell the biggest lie of the century while appearing like everything was together because I used to do it. This was where my doubt continued with Black. There was no way a woman would just leave a pregnancy test in a man's car unless that man was her baby's daddy. Still, I yearned to bet on us and our future to make everyone, especially Parri, wrong. All men weren't made of hot dogs from hell and fries. Not Black, and that was my hope. Therefore, in response to his I love you, I said, hiding all signs of doubt ...

"I love you, too. Sorry for hitting you."

"You hit like a girl." He responded in an I forgive you tone, and I took it as that. He had a way of saying things to put me at ease, letting me know the reason that I fell in love with him in the first place. When he hung up the phone, I walked inside to a dancing tenant.

"Jeena, I'm so glad to be free! My ass used to get beat and bruised, but now, I'm celebrating my freedom. I don't have any friends here, so please, be my first."

I moseyed over and sat down in front of the steak she so nicely laid on the rather exquisite plate she provided. The plate was heavily garnished with a T-bone dead center, and I wasn't going to make the mistake and not eat it. I laid down a prayer to dismiss any poison, and I ate. She was right. It was delicious.

"What did you marinate this in, Lynia? It's fantastic. Oh my gosh! You've got to give me the recipe."

"No can do. An old grandmother's secret, and I swore that I would never let up off of it - ever. You and your man can come over any time, or I'm free to deliver. Knock off five dollars for rent..."

I coughed. I knew it was too good to be true. I didn't even swallow. Instead I reached over to grab a napkin to spit it out. I'm getting my rent. The devil is a liar, and her butt believed his lies obviously when it came down to my money.

"No! No! Just kidding! Damn, you were about to spit all that goodness out," she exclaimed, snatching the napkins off the table. "Didn't I sign the contract? I joke a lot, so take me seriously, not so much."

Lynia had this big bun on the top of her hair with strands of hair rushing down to her shoulders. The strands were so straight that it looked like they were in a rush to get away from her head. She appeared biracial, but of what races, I couldn't decide. She brought out the best of both the Chinese and Black worlds, however, she could have easily been Cuban with a touch of soul and spark of something else.

"What's your background, as far as family?"

"You mean my race?"

"Yeah, because if I guess, it would be a guess of Black and Asian."

"Well, you're only half right. The other half of me is I have no earthly idea."

"Really?"

"Yep. Mom is black, and you know how the story goes with men, well, the men in my life. They're just dogs, dopes or ditching. My mom won't talk about him at all. To tell you the truth, I don't think mom even knows, so I can't be too hard on him without telling her that she should have been less loose about her legs. Overall, I could care less. I'm just glad I'm here, and thank them and the Man upstairs for getting me here." She sat down at the table. "So what's your story?"

"My story?" I stopped chewing, feeling that knot in the bottom of my stomach created by dragging my past up to anyone. I wasn't one of those people who are too proud of the wrong I've done, so it wasn't like I was so anxious to share. That voluntary sharing thing would've had to wait until I got older, wiser and just didn't give a rip.

"Yeah, you had your man issues," she continued without me volunteering what she considered my story. "The one thing I've found out is that it's so freeing to find a friend who you can relate to and one who can relate to you."

Friends? We're friends now? I uncomfortably responded while ripping up the steak before me, "True." Then I went silent. When I looked back up, she was still there waiting on me to dish my end of the bad romance.

"Well, I had sex with the wrong man, and he tried to kill me. The end."

"All over sex? There was no relationship?"

"Yeah, I mean, I'm not a woman that gets around or anything. We had a relationship," I looked back behind her at the patio doors which reminded me of how he broke in on me and beat me down. Then, I snapped out of it and continued talking. "But he's in jail now, and that's the end of it."

"You prosecuted him?"

"Uhm hmm." I wished she would shut up now. If she wanted names, dates and phone records, she wasn't getting it. That's why I should have never stopped in here for this lunch steak, but who passed on T-bones?

"I didn't do anything to my ex, but I'm thinking that I should have. You see this tooth?" She opened her mouth and showed me the only gleaming white one of the bunch. "This is the fake one. He knocked it out. Of course, I took a hammer to his back and ran, so we were over at that point. I walked around looking like sore mouth for about two weeks. It was horrible."

"Well, thank you so much for the steak," I stated gratefully as I swigged down the iced water not wanting to know anymore about her or vice versa, "But I really have to go now. That's my appointment calling." Immediately in my mind, I thanked God for Tanya who'd just started vibrating my phone.

"Okay, well we'll do this again sometime. Take one to your husband," she offered, wrapping another steak up. I was impressed with her social attitude, but I'd already allowed her to get too familiar with me, thus, it was breakout time.

I smiled while putting the phone up to my ear as I heard Tanya on the other end. "Thank you so much," I thanked Lynia as I took the succulent steak. "Don't lose your key!"

"Sure won't, and thanks again."

I was glad that was over. Tanya was patiently waiting on me to speak, but I wanted to be further away from my car before I started to talk. When I reached my car, my lips parted and words began to come out.

"What are you doing?" she asked.

"I came by your place earlier, but you weren't there so I left to just ride around and drop something off. How about you? Where've you been?"

"Girl, I had to go to the store and then turn in a job application. What I need is a computer so I can hit submit via the web like most people in my generation do. Tony told me you came by."

At that, I quickly sat inside my car and shut the door. This was going to be really hard. Parri had already warned me to let the junk die, bury itself and deform, but I couldn't just let myself be a matron of honor at her wedding without informing her about her man's misdeeds.

Facing the windshield, as I watched Lynia wave from the window, I spoke up slowly. "That's what I had to talk to you about, amongst other things, but the main thing is this." I backed up, losing focus of my crazy tenant from the window to ensure a clear path behind the car. "It's about Tony."

"Lord, Jeena, I don't want to hear it, okay?" she whined. "I already know he's not perfect and neither am I, so..."

"It's not about you though. As a matter of fact, it isn't about perfection either. It's about a situation that happened that you may need to be made aware of, only if you want to be made aware. Perfection and mistakes and all that have nothing to do with it, Tanya. It has to do with respect and honor after you marry him."

"What the hell!" she yelps. "I can't get a man without some bum ass news!" She was ticked. Her voice was on nine, and ten was the highest number. Instead of driving behind a tree, getting out and burying myself, I just opened my mouth and let the bad news come pouring out.

"When I went to your apartment, Tanya, I didn't go inside..."

"Well, that's new because Tony told me you came in and sat down for some time before you left."

This was another reason why she needed to listen and take her hot temper down to the cool, summer days of single-dome. Her man was a full out cheating liar, and he would have slept with me if he had the chance.

"He lied, Tanya, and if your cell phone was actually on, then I would have been able to tell you that before he filled your ears with garbage and tree sap."

"So you weren't inside?"

"No, Tanya. That's not the problem though."

"I already know."

"Excuse me?"

"I already know, so you don't have to tell me. He told me first."

"Well, what did he say?"

"He said that he came on to you, but you told him off and left. He said he's sorry, so I forgive him. I told him that my friends don't stab me in my back like that. They may tell it like it is, but at least they're up front."

Say what? Then why the heck was she with him? It would seem she would want that same respect from her man who is also supposed to be her number one friend.

"So he did tell you."

"Yep, and he's learning that I prefer to know things from him than to walk up on it."

"That doesn't make it cool, Tanya!" I was frustrated. She didn't understand that just because someone tells you that they're about to slit your throat doesn't make it okay to do just because they told you up front. "What part of that ain't okay don't you understand? He came and snatched my phone out of my hand when I was about to call the law on him for harassment. That's probably the real reason why he turned that lie he told you into the truth, scared I would follow through."

"What the hell you do that for? He's on probation, Jeena. There are plans in my future with him you know."

"Any fool with eyes can see that that he's on probation. He even warned me not to tell you, but look at me now, being the friend and all, but you're not even appreciating it."

"Jeena, now who said I wasn't appreciative? Truth is," she paused, "and you can't tell anyone. You better promise to God."

Oh no. Not another secret. I can't. "No, I'm not promising, Tanya..."

"No this one, I need you to because I'm not really marrying that asshole for no damn love. Get a clue, Jeena. When I said I have plans just now, I mean I really do have plans, girl!" she squealed. "I wouldn't have cared if you sexed him either because he's about to get fucked over by me, and I'm so happy I could scream! I've had to fake this in love with him thing for this long in front of everyone just so I can pull it off."

What? She could have fooled me. I really thought she was in love, but what could she possibly want with the freaking future jailbird? I wanted to know what she had going on so I responded, "I promise." My voice dragged because I had a feeling this was going to get me caught up into something I didn't want to be in. She started to spill the beans.

"Money."

"He's broke, Tanya. If you don't watch it, you will be, too."

"Where do you think I got all that new stuff from, Jeena? My damn job? Hell no. It was him. He has gobs of it. Once I say I do, maybe even before that, that shit is mine, too. I'm gonna get that weed smoking, drug dealing thief locked up and all that loot is mine and my kids. He can drop the soap in prison when I get done with his dumb ass. Cheat on me hell. Watch. All mine. Joke's on him. How ya' like being played?"

"No kidding?"

"No jokes. Plus," she changed her voice to a whisper. "I can get him popped for murder. First degree. His ass is gone. I got the proof. That fucker was talking on the phone to his conspirator, and I recorded that shiiiiitt! That's why I always let my phone go off so he won't ask me for it. Trust me, I got this. And girl, he has thousands!"

"You're shacking up with a flipping murderer, Tanya! Are you flipping out of your mind!" I wasn't impressed. She was risking her life for a load of cash, and that crap was lethal to her health. There wasn't that much backstabbing in the world.

"Fact is, if I can help it, there isn't even going to be a ceremony. Watch. One of my plans is to legalize the marriage first, like in a couple weeks or sooner if I can talk him into it, then turn that evidence in to the cops. Boom! He'll think I'm torn up sad, but really, I'll be super happy that there is no ceremony with a bed full of cash atop an annulment! All his extra chicks get no more of that money while all I have to do is be certain he goes away for thirty to life. Boom!"

My mouth remained open, drying itself up like a dehydrator was sitting inside of it, as I eyed the phone as if it wasn't even my own. This chick was for real, and not an inkling of fear, anxiety or dread came through in her voice. She was flippin' ecstatic!

"Don't go all quiet. Wait until your man puts you through hell, that wrong will look and feel so right. My kids have to eat, and I'm truly tired of the stamps. They don't buy clothes and a nice home. You are the only person in the world that knows my plan, so don't say shit or my throat might get cut."

So much for my thinking that Tanya was forgiving without something up her sleeve. Too bad for me that I was the only person in the world who knew her plan. She had to have that under wraps because the one thing I knew was that she could lose everything, maybe even her life, if she let the cat out of the bag, with me stuck in the middle. If Tony ever found out that I knew, I was done, especially after the stunt I pulled today. He would swear up and down that we both conjured this madness up, and I wanted no parts of it. I wasn't scared of him by any means, but treachery like this was bound to get a butt or two kicked.

"Are you sure you want to do this, Tanya? That man will get mad as hell if he finds out."

"Find out from where? You?"

Her voice cut straight through me like she was saying *try it, Jeena, just try it*. She had nothing to worry about on my end. That was her business, and a plot as thick as the one she was concocting, I wanted no parts of although it was as legal as ever. The only crime she committed was recording someone say he committed a murder, but what cop or prosecutor would really lock her up? I hated to admit it, but she hit a goldmine.

"Be careful, Tanya. Don't talk to me about this nonsense again, though, because this is the second time you're dragging me into something."

"Oh stop being so scary. Anyway, how are you and Stay?"

I didn't say a word as I watched the mileage of my car scroll down to another number.

"Hello?" she beckoned as I stalled, and I knew she'd catch on to the fact that something was dead wrong. Therefore, I said it - kinda.

"You know what? My bad, Tanya, I was making a turn and almost hit a vehicle." I asked forgiveness for that lie fast. "I just left a friend of mine's place," And I asked again. "And she was asking me about her man cheating, but she had no proof because all she found was a pregnancy test."

"Shut up, Jeena!"

"No seriously," I said matter of factly. I had no idea that this would come next from her mouth.

"Black got somebody pregnant?"

My Life Became A Nightmare.

From learning about a murder plot to both Parri and Tanya getting together behind my back to talk about my own husband shoving DNA into another woman, my life became full of vomit. I was literally throwing up in the toilet and feeling sick as a dog. Parri and Tanya called me over and over again, individually and as a three way connection, trying to find out each and every detail of a conversation I had yet to have with Black as follow up to the pregnancy test fiasco. To top that off, Faith was calling, too!

Fact was, that I was semi-happy to accept Black's excuse of I don't know how the pregnancy test got there, but then he came home.

"Back up, baby, please," Black stated with tears in his eyes as I met him at the door, teeth brushed and vomit free. "Just go, Jeena. In the house, please," he begged.

Black was pushing my arms away from him, forcing me back inside, and I didn't know what was up until I looked outside beyond the blinds that he was in the process of closing. When I saw what I saw, I lost it. My whole religion went out the window. I snapped.

"What the fuck was that?" I fumed. Feeling my tongue getting bombarded with curse words, my mouth felt like lead, but as they streamed out, my tongue felt as light as a feather. I was out of control. "What the hell is sprayed all over your car, Black? Answer me! And get the fuck off of my arm!" I yelled, pulling away from him, but he grabbed me and pulled me back tighter, staring me in my face, the tears breaking free from his eyes.

"I don't know, Jeena," he stammered. "I went outside after work, and there it was. I closed the place down. Sent everyone home, and I parked where I normally do. Man, Jeena, this looks bad, but I'm telling you I don't have any other woman in my life."

My eyes burned through his skin as he blocked me from the window and the door while I was in a constant struggle to leave the house and see just what the hell I was missing. Finally, he let me go, and I walked outside.

The car was sprayed with yellow spray paint, a color you can't miss. Before we got married, for his birthday, it was me who laid down cash money to get his car repainted when I needed my own car painted over. As I walked up closer to his car, I read the word BITCH on one side, and then as I walked over to the other side of the car, ASS was sprayed in bright orange with pink hearts all over it. Whoever it was even painted the tires green with red hubcaps. Hell, it looked ten times worse than mine!

I turned back to see Black at the door, and my spirit broke down to nothing. I just wept. It was a female, and she was scorned like a mug by my one and only husband.

"Fuck you!" I yelled at Black as I walked back into the house. He wiped his face and came after me, but I was already headed toward the bathroom to eliminate my closet of my clothes because I was moving out until he got his trick under control. Before I could grab the first item, Black jumped in front of me, blocking my path.

"Jeena, what is wrong with you?" he yelled. "I took a bullet for you and this bullshit outside on the car or some fake pregnancy test is gonna make you walk the hell up outta here on me?" When I didn't answer, he grabbed my arm to try and hold me still to force me to listen, but, I pulled my arm back and shoved him as hard as I could, so hard that he slammed into the wall. "Jeena, answer me, baby. Come on, I took a bullet for you, baby," he continued, his voice quivering and weak from not knowing what to say or do to make me calm down.

"I never asked you to come and take a mother fuckin' bullet for me! Never! Not damn once!" I screamed while the tears streamed down my face as Black's face took on a rage of its own. "And even if you did take a bullet for me, it doesn't give you the right to cheat on me and get another woman pregnant."

"You think this doesn't bother me?" He yelled, slamming his fist against a large fist pump statue, causing it to fall and break into pieces while it drew blood from his knuckles. "Do you really think I didn't want to fuckin' hurt somebody today knowing I had to come back home for you to see this shit?" His nostrils were flaring like a bull, and his dreadlocks were scattered. His work suit wasn't put together on his body anymore, but instead, the tie was loose while I even spotted some paint on the side of his pants.

I just stood there in my stretch jeans and summer shirt in tears as he tried to explain his side of the story which was nothing. Absolutely nothing. Everything that came from his mouth was an *I don't know who* and *I don't know what* until I just asked him politely to get out of my way.

"Please, Black, move." Those words strained me to no end, but I had to get them out because there was no way karma was going to drag me down like it did Tina. There was no way in heaven I was going to let it do me the way I did her, not without getting out of the crap at the beginning. I didn't want to suffer. I didn't want the pain of it all. I wanted to get out while my heart could still take it and not hate the one thing that I'd come to appreciate and know – love.

Black, before my very eyes, got down on his knees and stared me in my face. "I almost died for you, Jeena. There is no other woman. I promise you, baby. I even put my neck on the line and asked the owner of the company today if she accidentally dropped a test in my car the other day, and baby, that's not something you just ask the owner of the company. That's that drama, Jee." Black then stood back up to look me straight in the eyes. "It wasn't hers, Jeena. It wasn't…and I don't know what's going on or how…"

As his hands flew up in the air at a loss for words, I interjected before my heart overtook my mind. "I just have to get out of here, Black. I can't make sense of it. I have to go." I stared down at the floor. "Not for good. Just for now. I have to leave," I stressed.

During my stressed out moment, Black leaned over, caressed the back of my neck and placed his lips atop mine, passionately kissing me. With tears on full stream down my cheeks, I kissed him back. I wanted to love him, but not like this - not with spray paint on his car and pregnancy tests hidden in the passenger's car door pocket. I just wanted it to be us, and it was us, for that moment.

Black's hands rubbed me up my bare back as he reached the top to loosen the straps, and my shirt fell down to the floor. There I stood, nothing on except my jeans and heels as I rubbed Black's suit jacket onto the floor. His tie, I eased off while he unzipped my jeans, and his shirt, I unbuttoned until there was nothing left to unbutton – slacks, too. He was all there for me, just me. At that moment, there was no hidden woman because Black placed me on the bed, pulled off my jeans, and made love to me like I was the only woman in his life and…

<u>In The World.</u>

"What do you mean you left? Like left left?"

"Yeah, I'm gone as of…" I glanced down at the cell phone clock, "now."

I had only been four hours since Black made love to me like I was the last drink of water in a dry, barren land. It took every bone in my young body to not stay there and just believe him. The fact was that evidence was sprayed on his car and positive tests were dumped there as well, making me the dummy for even thinking this was possibly all a bad joke.

"Where are you gonna live?"

"Well, I'm not gone forever, Faith. At least I hope not, but like I just told you, what else was I supposed to do? Stick around to find out when the next avalanche was gonna hit?"

"Where are you off to?"

"A hotel."

"I'm coming. Which hotel? No sister of mine is going to be alone during a time like this. Tell me which hotel?"

"I don't know," I answered as frustrated as I'd ever been, sexually, mentally and emotionally. I was done. "The Cinco Rays, I guess. It's only thirty minutes away from you, so it'll be a half and half trip for us."

"Okay, when I get there, I'll call you. Drive safe, sis, and you know I have you in prayer. This is going to work out fine, in Jesus' name."

"In Jesus' name," I responded in agreement because I really did want my marriage to work, with or without the hang-ups. Before she hung up, I caught her. "Faith, oh yeah. I cussed him out. I kinda slipped on my good behavior. I feel bad, really bad. I feel like my salvation..."

"Stop right there. Your salvation is fine. You made an error in anger. Jesus still loves you, and the fact that you feel bad about it says that you aren't proud and repentant. Ask for forgiveness and when you face Black again, things will be better than ever. You aren't perfect, but Jesus is for you. Do better next time. See you soon."

"Thanks, little sis. Later." She always knew what to say. If I didn't know any better, I would claim she was my little angel.

My car smelled like the food I had in it earlier today. I had no idea why the smell was still lingering when it wasn't even in the car that long until I saw that it wasn't the fast food smell. Instead it was juice from the steak that Lynia sent for Black. She put it inside the foil, and I forgot to go back out to the car and wipe what wasted out. Who did that? Foil wasn't supposed to hold fluid, but it was obvious Lynia didn't know that.

My phone rang. Glancing down at it revealed Parri on the other end, so I hit speaker. "Yeah?"

"Yeah? What's wrong with you? I thought I asked you to call me back about you and Black. You know me and Tanya have been trippin' right now over this..."

"Save your words, Parri."

"Why?"

"I'm on my way to The Cinco Rays for the night or maybe even two nights."

"Oh shoot, Jeena. It's his, ain't it?"

"It sure looks that way. Look, Parri, can I just drive?"

"Yeah, you can drive, but I'm bringing the pizza, subs and soda with a big bottle of wine. Bye."

"Parri!" I yelled but it was too late. I knew I would see her at the hotel as well. It looked like it was going to be a full out girl's retreat, and although I didn't want it, I also didn't want to stop it either. Wait until they find out about his ride.

"It was the whole car, Jeena?"

"Yeah, Parri." My head was throbbing. I felt like I was in the twilight zone or the Bermuda Triangle. As a matter of fact, I wished I was there so I could disappear and find my way back when the dust settled and I could care less. Emotions were a pain in the butt! If you loved, you got hurt, and if you didn't love, you were missing something on the inside. I couldn't live with emotions well, and I never could live without them. I just had to find out how to deal with them, but make good decisions.

Black called my phone twice since I left the house, and I didn't pick those calls up either. As bad as I wanted to, I just couldn't. I was in love, but I didn't like him at the moment because I didn't know if he was the truth or a lie. There was absolutely nothing worse than trying to figure out if something was real or fake, so I just preferred to leave it where it was, letting it sort itself out. I was just about done.

"Parri, the car was a wreck on the outside. There were hearts and everything drawn on it, like a woman who was truly scorned." There was a knock at the door during my conversation with Parri who sat on the hotel bed with me shoving a piece of pizza in her mouth like she was watching a drama unfold at the movie theater. Here I was again, the plot point of this year's controversy. "This must be Faith." I rolled off the bed to answer it, and just as planned, it was my little sister.

"Jeena," she sighed, "Girl, I had to stop for gas, and then realized I didn't have my wallet in my purse, so I had to turn around and go get it. That's why I'm so late," she explained, waltzing into the room. "Oh, hi, Parri. How are things?"

"Not too good. Go ahead and tell her, Jeena, about all the paint and piss and whatever else goes onto a pregnancy test because I've never had to take one."

Faith and I just glanced at Parri in disgust, but ended up forgetting about it as usual because we knew just how blunt she carried herself. As far as Faith, she wasn't on top of her fashions as usual when it came to spur of the moment outings. She had the nerve to really walk into the lobby of this hotel wearing curlers in her hair, a cute pair of house shoes, but still, they were house shoes, jogging pants and an oversized shirt that read *I'll see you in heaven*. I loved the Lord very much, but my sister was a walking billboard for Jesus wherever she went. I wasn't mad at her for that, but the house shoes and the curlers were a bit much.

"I already know about the pregnancy test, Parri," she said, turning her attention back to me, "but what about this paint? I thought you left over the test, not paint, sis? What's up?"

I flopped onto the bed and buried my face into the plush pillow. Then, while muffled, I answered, "Some scorned woman that I think he was sleeping with spray painted his car all over – B.I. T. C. H. A. S. S." I spelled it to keep myself from adding insult to the injury I did back at the house. "Even the tires were colorful. Sorry I didn't tell you on the phone the whole reason why things blew over."

Faith came to sit down beside me as she started to rub my back. I was a useless blob of skin at this point. I just wanted to shut my eyes and dream for three days straight, probably ask God for that same whale He got to swallow up Jonah to do me the same favor.

"Did he tell you who it was?"

"No. He said that he didn't know. He was even crying, raging mad, but nothing. He could tell me nothing. Now what's that? A woman spraying your car, an anonymous pregnancy test all in the same week, and all I get is an *I don't know?*"

"No, sis. He has to know something, at least that's what it seems. Let's just eat, pray and get your mind off of this madness." Faith reached for a slice of pizza and turned on the television. "It's going to be alright, and your marriage is going to last through this. You hear me? He loves you. Trust that. He took a bullet. He saved your life and took a bullet. He can't be a bad guy. Maybe he could have clouded judgment at times, but not a bad guy."

She was right. I just didn't know if I could be in love with him back through this. Just as I was gathering myself together, Parri hopped up from the bed to answer her cell phone. I took the remote to search for a good movie, and Faith went inside the bathroom to change clothes because she drove here ready to talk and get in the bed. That all changed when I heard Parri in a Father God moment.

"Oh Jesus! Oh Jesus, Tanya, what's wrong. Breathe, girl, breathe!"

"Help me, please," Tanya choked as Parri placed her on speaker. I rose up from bed flushed with fear when I heard Tanya's voice. I'd never heard her this way, and I shot over to Parri as she leaned over the phone while it sat atop the hotel's empty icebox.

"What's wrong?" Parri yelled. "Don't say help! Who is there, what's happening?" Parri was going frantic because in the background we heard stuff being thrown around in the background, but no voices until when Tanya screamed and the phone dropped, hitting something that was more than likely the floor.

"Faith! Faith!" I screamed as I jumped to my cell on the bed to call 911, so that I could send them to Tanya's address.

She was being attacked, had to be, and all her children were probably inside the apartment with her.

Faith came running out of the bathroom frantically already undressed and in her pajamas. "What? What is it?"

"It's Tanya, we gotta go. Hello...I need the police or ambulance to go to..." In the middle of my call for help, Parri rushed to the phone and snatched away.

"Don't ever call the cops Tanya's way! You don't know who's gonna be arrested, Jee, damn! Let's go now. Why do you think she called us? Don't you think 911 is much easier, Jee, huh? You want her to lose her kids?"

"No, Parri!" I snapped back. "I don't want her to lose her life! You heard her on the phone!"

Faith immediately interjected calmly. "Let's just go." She grabbed her keys, and we all followed her out of the door as she started into hard and heavy prayer, walking down the corridor in her pajamas with no shimmy or shame. I followed suit while Parri hustled to the door repeating *Jesus* and *Amen*.

Before we got through the lobby, Parri'd already rushed to get her car to the front of the double doors, and we jumped in – Faith in her pajamas and me with just my cell phone. It was about to be a long night because it'd already felt like we were too late for saving Tanya from whatever it was she needed saving from.

I thought back to the secret she told me to keep about her man Tony having murdered someone while also stashing loads of cash, and I wondered if she'd slipped up in her plan. It was highly possible because she'd already gotten confident by letting me in on it, but even though this situation seemed volatile, I couldn't let the girls know. No way, at least not yet.

"Can you drive any faster?" I asked Parri.

"Just call her back. Keep calling until she picks up, Faith. Here, just keep hitting redial." She tossed the phone into Faith's lap, and Faith got to it, over and over and over again like Tanya's life depended on it. So far, for all we knew, it did depend on it. If the cops got involved, who knew what would happen, so we had to hurry.

I sat back and shut my eyes. Tears began to flow down once again as I thought about not just Tanya but my own life that was falling apart. The word to believe was that bad things happen, but who knew they would go from good to terrible in a matter of seconds?

"I can't believe this. Tanya's being attacked right after my husband and I split for a minute, and even during the wedding I couldn't catch a break," I stated in the worst I'm giving up on life tone I could muster.

As Parri drove, she asked about what I said, proving that she can multitask extremely well. That was one thing about her, she missed absolutely nothing. While Faith, she probably heard me as well, but she was one to prioritize her follow-ups.

"Jeena, what do you mean during the wedding you couldn't catch a break? Your damn wedding..." She quickly caught herself because most people really respect the God in Faith. Parri really didn't realize that Faith paid that talk no mind at that moment because like I said, Faith prioritized well. "I'm sorry, Faith. My fault. Your wedding went smoothly from what I could tell."

"That's what you think. That's what everyone thought," I said making it a point to let everything hang out since I was fairly certain that my marriage was already in the tubes rolling down. "I got a note, like a card, in an envelope. As I was walking down the aisle, I picked it up off the last chair, and the lady that left it was already walking away. I didn't recognize her at all, but to make a long story short, it was a threat."

"A threat?" Parri asked, running the stop sign.

"Yeah. It basically told me that this S.H.I.T. ain't over."

"What was that supposed to mean?"

I opened my eyes to meet Parri's eyes staring right at me and not the road through the rear view mirror. "What do you mean, what was that supposed to mean? It looked like someone, like Andre' or hired by Andre', was trying to shake me down and break me down so that I could look over my shoulder. It was some obvious retaliation for him getting locked up."

"What did Black say?"

"He doesn't know."

"He doesn't know?" Faith chimed in. Now that the conversation got more serious, she chimed in.

"No, he doesn't. I just felt like I owed him at the time, to give him a good honeymoon. Anyway, I kept the card, and after I'd put it out of my mind, I ran into it again..."

"That's messed up, Jeena. I wouldn't take it lightly though. A threat is a threat, and after what happened to you, you should be on high alert. I mean, what if all that's happening has to do with that note? You really should consider that, Jeena, and then let Black know before doing anything else."

"I can't believe you didn't tell me that, Jeena!"

"Faith, I didn't want you to worry. I'm fine. Do you see?" I raised and waved my arms and fingers so that she could see that I was alive. "I'm still here. Besides that, I kept the note just in case something did go down. And, Parri, this stuff between me and Black has nothing to do with the note. A pregnancy test in his car and spray paint all over his car? That hardly has anything to do with that note."

"It only sounds far fetched, but maybe that's the whole idea, Jeena. Think like a psycho. If you think like a psycho, you'll find the psycho. You told me that Black did swear up and down that he didn't know."

I was sick of this, so I screamed, "And what man wouldn't deny it? Tell me now, but I highly doubt any man would claim a random pregnancy test." I glared back at Parri in the mirror, and she politely put her eyes back onto the road. Faith started to redial Tanya's place while I just sat back once again and cried. This night was going to …

<u>Hell.</u>

We rushed into a parking space in front of Tanya's apartment, and by that time I was all dried up and ready for action. I'd gotten overwhelmed inside the car, and it boiled over onto Parri who was just trying to help. When I got out of the car, I walked over to her and said sorry near her ear. She rolled her eyes and said whatever, but I knew that meant things were fine.

There were no cops in the yard and absolutely no sign of anything odd on the street, therefore, we gathered that the commotion was contained inside the apartment. We'd rushed over to Tanya's, but we were hesitant about knocking on the door, afraid of what we might encounter on the other side. The only thing we did was look at each other and listened for noise coming from the freshly painted black door, but there was nothing. There wasn't even any noise from the children which caused my heart to sink to the lowest level humanly possible. I knew I used to call them children of the corn, but I really used to love them all – corn or no corn.

Faith's eyes began to get red as she tried to remain strong while Parri continued to shake her hands out and take deep breaths as to get ready for action. We were dumb enough not to stop off and get something like a bat, spatula or hammer just in case, so it was just our loud screams, hands and feet that were going to get us through this with Jesus. Fact was, Jesus was all we needed.

"You ready?" Parri asked.

"Call her one more time, Faith," I requested.

Faith started to dial as we stood there, but there was still no answer. Our breathing froze in hopes that Tanya picked up, but the answering machine began to speak instead. We only had two choices at this point – call the cops or kick it in. Before that though, I squeezed my body in between Faith and Parri to turn the rusted knob, the most un-kept looking thing about this apartment, and the door opened. My fingers loosened their grasp on the knob, and Faith tapped the door with her finger.

As the door swung open, it was like a ghost town. No one was in sight, but the place definitely looked haunted. Items were tossed to and fro, from one side of the living dining room combo to the other. The clock that hung on the wall, which I noticed on my first visit here, was in pieces, glass on the floor with some pieces tainted with what looked like blood. My stomach weakened, and immediately, I began to sob.

"Hold it together. Both of you," Faith encouraged us. "Nobody's here. I'm walking back," she whispered in reference to the rooms down the hall.

"To get yourself killed? We need to leave!" I argued in a low tone, and Parri backed me up on my decision.

"That's right. We can't just walk in here because what if the worst is back there? Then we have all this blood on our shoes, Faith. Let's back up. It was my fault. We should have called the cops back at the hotel," Parri stated as she started to break down.

"I'm calling the cops, and I'm letting them know that I'm at the scene of a crime. You two stay here." She started to dial, but I followed her each step to the hallway as Parri stood watch from the front door. I wasn't going to let my sister walk back to the back and get killed over some ignorance. What they didn't know was that Tony wasn't just a man, he was a murderer on the loose.

"Wait a minute, Faith. Keep talking to the operator," I pulled her arm back. I was her older sister. If anyone was going to catch a beat down first, it was going to be me. I couldn't take Tony, but I would sure try. I knew Faith would have my back because she was afraid of nothing. Ye though she walk through the valley of the shadow of death, she would fear no evil – just like the Bible stated. She feared nothing. As for me, I was just now getting there...literally in the moment that I turned the corner into what looked like Tanya's bedroom.

She had the same mirror hanging over the head of her bed, given to her by her great grandmother. It was a family heirloom she told me, and there was still no spot or crack on it, despite what I saw in the front room. The covers were drawn back on the queen bed, neatly, but there was something odd about the scene. All the drawers from the dresser were pulled open and the clothes didn't look dumped but placed on the side of the dresser intact. It was like they were just being rearranged.

Faith remained on the phone, talking to the operator, telling her each step we were taking to find Tanya. It was time for me to turn into the master bathroom. The tan door was ajar, and near the bottom of it, there were more traces of blood, and I started to tremble, remembering back to when I was in this same position, only I got out alive. My breathing began to go faint as I placed my right foot on the door and lightly pushed it open. There was even more blood, and instead of talking to the 911 operator, Faith kept the phone to her ear and went into a deep prayer. She was right. We needed Jesus more than anything before the cops because as I pulled back the shower curtain, following the blood trail, there was Tanya, passed out with the phone in her hand, naked from the top up.

"Oh Jesus, Lord help us please," I faintly stated, falling on my knees at the tub to check her pulse near her neck which was completely layered in blood. She was still alive. "She's still alive! She's still alive! Send somebody!" I screamed at the phone in Faith's hand, and about five seconds later, Parri showed up at the bathroom door, grabbing her chest as she ended up vomiting into the sink at the sight of Tanya.

"Come fast please, send someone fast. It looks like someone tried to kill her. She's bleeding, losing blood fast, but she has a pulse. Apply pressure to where the blood is coming from, Jeena, the operator says."

Immediately, I snatched a towel from the hanger, leaned over her, and pressed the opening at the side of her neck. Jesus, they'd tried to kill her. Tony, he'd tried to kill her.

"Where are the kids? Go find the kids, Parri, go!" Instead of sadness overwhelming me, I was finding a rage, a panic filled rage, that was escalating by the second. If those kids were dead, I did believe that I would need some serious counseling after I go postal on whoever did it. "Do it now. Look everywhere." I turned back to face a passed out, near death Tanya. "Don't worry. We're finding the kids. I know you trained them well. They're not stupid. They're alive somewhere. They're alive. You stay alive, too, because they want their mother. You hear me? They want their mom."

The blood started to trickle down my wrist as I tired from pressing, so Faith grabbed the only other towel in the bathroom and handed it to me. Simultaneously, Parri came like a lightning bolt into the bathroom.

"The kids must have gone out of the window, but I found the baby. I found the little baby. The window is open, but when I opened up the closet, there was a foot moving around. It's the baby. Tanya, we have your baby. She's alive. On your bed. She's alive. I'm gonna go feed her. She's so happy. I'm going to get the milk, okay, until you get cleaned up. I'm taking care of the little bit."

Parri was rambling in efforts to trigger more fight to live inside of Tanya, and I could tell she was fighting with all her might along with Faith who was busy ignoring the operator on her knees in prayer. If the operator said something worth answering, that was the only time Faith would break her prayer to answer. Other than that, Jesus was coming in the room tonight, and Tanya was going to be alright.

"No storm, Lord, no storm can disturb your calm. Be with her, Jesus. Please have mercy and forgive her for any and all sins, and deliver her from this end. Restore Tanya, Father God. I beg you though we don't deserve your mercy, I beg you for it...for her and her children and for myself who is praying this prayer. Keep them, Jesus," Faith continued.

After two minutes of silence surrounding Faith's continuous prayer, there was a commotion coming down the hallway. It was the cops and the medical personnel. Faith rushed to pick up the telephone and moved away from me as I remained holding the towels on her neck. When I saw the help with my own eyes, I motioned to them with my free hand to come and take over.

I didn't move too far away, but sat down on the toilet and watched as they lifted Tanya from the tub and eventually onto the stretcher. Blood covered the tub. There was so much blood that if I didn't truly believe in the life saving power of Jesus Christ, I would have believed she would die. In my heart, mind and soul, however, I knew for a fact she would live. If God saved me last year from a stab near my heart, He wouldn't just let her go either, not like this. I trusted Him.

Walking into the bedroom from the bathroom was a huge task as I listened to them take her out of the house. I just sat down on the bed, but then I was interrupted by the police who quickly moved me to where Faith and Parri already stood. They watched as I was led up to the front door, blood covering my shirt and hands. From the side, Tanya's baby crying startled me, and I jumped to try to help the officer handle the small infant. It wasn't going to happen though. We weren't allowed to be in the apartment anymore. We had to answer...

Many Questions.

After the near murder scene, they were on a search for Tony. We didn't know for sure if Tony was the person who attacked Tanya, but he was definitely the prime suspect, especially after I talked to the cops. I'd told them everything about what Tanya told me. Well, I'd left out the part about her plot to rob him. I told them everything else...that she'd heard him say he murdered someone while he was talking on the phone amongst other things. It wasn't the other things that peeked their interest. It was only the suspicion of one murder and this possible attempted one that they were gunning for.

The children were found down the road inside of a ditch underneath some leaves. When the cops found them, the report was that they were quieter than the sound of mice. They said that it was their favorite hiding spot, and that their mom told them to hide until someone finds them if anything ever happened. That was what they did, and they didn't move. The oldest son said that he hid the baby in the closet wrapped up and sleeping with the pacifier. He said that was the only thing he could do for her, and thank God he did the right thing for a boy his age. The best thing was that he was able to tell the officers who he saw striking his mom. It wasn't Tony.

My cell phone rang as I sat inside the hospital with Tanya's mom, the children, Faith and Parri. It was getting later and later, and even though I left Black back at the house, I wished he was here with me. I answered the phone.

"Hello?"

"Jeena."

I didn't say anything at that moment. Instead, I got up from my seat and moved to the other side of the waiting area, not wanting to bring my simple cheating drama to the forefront when there were weightier things to think and pray about.

"Black, Tanya was attacked bad. She was bleeding everywhere," I continued as my voice wouldn't stop quivering. "We went into her apartment, and she was lying inside the tub with her throat slit on one side..."

"What?" he interrupted, shock vibrating through his voice. "Where are you? Jeena, I'm coming to you. Tell me where you are."

"I'm all bloody, Black." My hands started to tremble as I thought about the last time I was this bloody, and I felt myself coming down with an anxiety attack. I sat down and began to take deep breaths to calm myself back down.

Black panicked. I could tell he was moving around in the room frantically by all the stuff I heard dropping on the floor. That was what would happen when he was looking for something in a rush, everything would end up tossed and on the floor.

"Jeena, baby, try to calm down. I'm not gonna leave you alone. Who's with you now, babe. Breathe, baby, breathe."

"Parri, Faith and Tanya's mom with her children. I think Parri might end up taking them to her house so they can wash up good and get a good night's sleep. The only one having issues right now is the oldest because he was shielding the other kids from the violence by shoving them out the window. He said he told them to go to the ditch while he hid the baby. He said it was too hot outside...the baby would have gotten too hot..." I started to cry. "I know it had to to do with Tony and drugs...had to!"

"Listen. Don't think backwards, Jeena. Let's move forward, okay. The children and even Tanya are fine, okay. Come on. Let's do what we do, think on good things. Let's follow what the Lord says now," he consoled, "including when it comes to us."

I didn't speak. It was time for me to listen to words that could calm me, and if they came from the man I thought was cheating on me, then so be it. I needed some guidance because I was about to pop.

"I understand how angry we both got today, you at me and me at an unexplainable situation. I can tell you, Jeena, that I love you, and I'll shout that anywhere I can. Everyone knows this. Everyone."

Tears just rolled. I was done. My head went into my lap as I listened to the music come on in Black's vandalized car from the other end of the phone. Quickly he turned it off so that he could hear me, but I wasn't trying to talk anymore. I wanted to pray. I needed Jesus to sort things out for me or just give me the wisdom to sort things out the right way. I needed a way to find out what was truth and what was a lie in my life because things weren't cut and dry anymore. That was what I thought marriage was supposed to be – cut and dry. All I got so far was threatening letters and a woman after my man, and that wasn't cut and dry. That was wet like blood. Even my shirt had the stains of Tanya's blood to prove that my life and those around me had taken a turn for the not so good.

"I'll see you when you get here," I told Black. "It's the same hospital, our hospital. We're on the third floor. I need to go pray."

"Cool. Do that, and I'll be praying with you."

I took the phone from my ear until I heard him say holler back at me. When I put the phone back to my ear, Black told me that he loved me.

"I love you, too." And I did. I really did love him. That was the more reason I needed to pray, so that I could make the right decision, not be hasty. That was what the Bible said, so I was going to try to do this portion right.

The women's restroom was clear across the other side of the waiting area which was huge. Besides us, there were only a couple of other people who appeared like they were about to die if they held their breath any more waiting for a doctor to come out of surgery with good news. When Tanya arrived at the hospital, not the doctors or anyone would allow us a back which was understandable. There was even a cop assigned to keep visitors out because of the fact that they wanted to keep Tanya safe from the perpetrator who was unknown and still out lurking. What they were waiting on was Tanya to wake up, so that she could give the full name of the attacker if she knew. Her son only could reveal so much about the incident or the man who sliced his mom on the neck because he didn't actually see that part happen.

As I entered the bathroom, it smelled like it was just cleaned. A strong garden scent filled the bathroom that, when mixed with the Lysol, made for an *I'm safe* odor. I walked into the middle of the floor, washed my hands and arms again, and instead of kneeling, I lifted my hands in prayer.

"Father God in the name of Jesus, I know I haven't been the world's perfect person, but I am trying to be a better person by thinking better, speaking better and acting better. Lord, I thank you for saving me, and I know sometimes I mess up, but I'm better than I was before. Please forgive me for my sins, and right now, I need your guidance. Tanya needs your healing. Shoot, it seems like we all need something all the time," I prayed frustrated with myself. "Will you please help us, comfort her mother and children, and heal her, allowing her to walk out of this hospital and not die. Also, I need help in my marriage. Teach me what to do in my situation, and how I distinguish between the truth and a lie. If not that, Lord, please distinguish the two for me plainly where it concerns my marriage. Amen."

After the prayer, I just stood there. The four walls reminded me of being trapped, and it was just like I felt inside my body. As much as I wanted to jump out and run into someone else's fascinating and beautiful life, I quickly realized that there was no such thing. Everyone I knew, whether or not they revealed it, had an issue, so if I jumped out and into another body, I would have just as much trouble as I had to start. I felt an immediate moment of clarity inside the bathroom that had to have come from God Himself, and it said that most times, if not all times, people need to gain wisdom and strength by going through the hard times because taking the easy way out isn't always the best route.

I thought about myself and Black and how I needed to get to the bottom of this whole pregnancy test, either through him or someone. A hotel wasn't where I was gonna be laying my beat down brain for more than a day, maybe two, so this mess had to end. On top of that, one of my best friends in the world came so close to dying tonight, and I didn't even know why. I did know that it had everything to do with Tony, whether the cops could verify it or not. This had old murderer Tony written all over it.

Just then, someone knocked on the bathroom, and I froze. It literally broke my prayer concentration, and then it broke even more when a foot started tapping the bottom of the door.

"Jeena," she whispered, "Is this you?"

I dropped my hands from my meditative state and answered, "Yeah, Parri." I wiped my eyes and opened the door. I was about to come out, but Parri just came right on inside. Then, she closed it while ensuring that she locked it tightly. Despite the feeling of discomfort I had, I decided not to make it a big deal because the look on Parri's face told me that she had a mouthful to spill.

"Listen up, and girl, you are going to flip out when you hear this," she sang in a low tone, shaking her head. "Scoot over a little bit because bathroom walls are no joke. Listen," she continued, readjusting herself away from the toilet. "Tanya's mom just opened her mouth and started talking. I didn't ask her any questions either. She just started."

I stared. Did she not see that I was into my own moment? As I stared, I noticed a brand new small herring bone bracelet around her wrist as she flung her arms back and forth about to explain this new news.

"Where did you get the bracelet? It's cute."

"Jeena," she stated once again as she noticed my watery eyes. "Tanya's going to be fine. The doctor came out for a quick second and let us know that things are touchy, but she looks like she will pull through. Luckily, you broke the flow of blood with pressure, so we really need to thank God for that. Oh," she stammered as she held out her wrist. "I found it on the floor out there. Cute huh?" she said in reference to the bracelet. I lifted my eyes, but didn't have the words for Parri at the time.

"But look," she paused, leaned in closer to my face and then started again, this time with her eyebrows raised. "Guess what dead beat ass Tony was into?"

Murder, I thought. Killing people and stashing cash was my next thought, but Parri answered her own question. Lucky for me.

"He was trafficking heavily, even using the low key apartment to keep things on the down low! There's no bank account, and he kept all his money on him. According to Tanya's mom, she thinks that someone came for him, but ended up getting Tanya who they thought was in on a whole deal gone bad. The bottom line is that this entire thing is about to blow up with Tanya in the middle of it."

"Well, it gets worse," I added. What the heck? It was going to come out anyway. "Tony is a verified, stone cold killer, and, Parri, please don't say squat to anyone about what I just said." I rolled my watery, red eyes, and suddenly regretted my forthcoming information.

"What?" Parri's eyes got as big as owl's, and right as I was about to leave the bathroom, she stopped me at the lock. "A killer? Who told you that? What the heck is she doing with a serial killer?"

I backed away from the door quickly and waved all ten of my fingers in front of her glossy eyes. "Nobody said serial killer, Parri!" I whispered, straining my throat so much that I started to cough. I grabbed my throat and swallowed in the best attempt that I could make to wet the dryness. "I said killer, that's all. Nothing serial about that statement. I never said he killed over and over and over again, did I?"

"My bad, but you know what I meant, girl! Tanya is in trouble, and ain't that much difference between a serial killer and a one man killer. They still kill, Jeena, and that means that even when she does leave the hospital, she's still in danger."

I thought about what Parri said, and she was right. As she moved from in front of the door, she placed her hand on her hip and gave me a Tanya's in serious trouble look no matter how we decided to look at it. The other thing was that if we decided to intervene, our lives could end up in the line of fire as well. I didn't like this. I didn't like this one bit. I didn't want to ask, but Tanya was going to tell me something. Maybe not the cops, but she was going to have to tell me...

What In The World Was Going On.

My feet dragged to the bathroom's mirror instead of opening the door. Parri came right up beside me, and as she did, I busted out crying again. I didn't even look at Parri standing there next to me because for some reason, I began to get

116

extremely angry, not about any situation, but at her. I was angry at her.

As she inched up about to touch me on my back as a gesture of comfort, I shrugged her off of me even though she hadn't touched me yet. I sensed her doing that same thing that she'd normally do at a time like this – say I told you so and then toss her hands back like *what did I do*? Honestly, I was angry because she was always right about people. I was so tired of it I could scream.

Finally, my eyes met hers and I fumed. "Why are you in here, Parri? Tanya is in the bed nearly killed, and you bring me news about her man, but you did it almost with a smile on your face. So go ahead and say it, Parri."

"Say what?"

There she was again, acting dumb.

"I told you so...or should I say, I told y'all so. Tony was altogether bad, and I suppose when Black comes up here, because he is coming, you'll run back to Tanya's mom and tell her about our split with a slight grin on your face, too, because you've never been through nothing because you happen to always be right!"

"Where the hell is this shit coming from? Fuck you, Jeena, and your lame ass argument over this dumb shit." She stuck her neck out again and opened her eyes wider with an even bigger grin on her face. Then she plastered all her teeth together so that I could see her pearly pink gums, and without moving her lips said, "Fuck you again, and I am always right. If her dumb ass...I love her...but if her dumb ass wasn't with him, she wouldn't be half dead now. All her ass had to do was run his ass out the house like she did last time with a damn shank, but instead, her ass got shanked." She wiped the grin from her face, and finished what she'd started, "And don't tell me one thing about going through because you don't know half the shit I deal with, including y'all dumb asses. Need to get out of your feelings so much and listen to facts. Stop getting so offended at true shit, defending your dumbness Reality is this – she isn't just your friend. I got her back more than you because I wasn't tiptoeing around telling her like it is!"

I wanted to slap her, but I already knew that she would slap me back. Really, I'd had enough licks in my lifetime, and secondly, I was afraid that my fake tits would pop out and leak from a beat down coming my way. I wasn't quite comfortable with the squish, fall, leak and flatten.

Parri's eyes didn't back up from mine. She was so close to my face that I couldn't breathe without smelling her breath. At that point, I wished I didn't have gum in my mouth and my breath smelled like rotten fish so I could blow up her nostrils and have her fall out. She was just lingering in my face, waiting on me to make my move, so I did.

"I'ma pray for you."

"Pray for me?" She jumped back and put her hand on her chest. That was my move. People hated it when you said that. It's worse than a cuss word. To say I'm gonna pray for you in an argument was like saying they have a demon on their back or they need Jesus because they really don't have Him right. People, saved and unsaved, hated that accusation of imperfection, even though they knew that they were nowhere near perfect. No one was.

I smiled this time. Ha flippin' ha. Lord, please forgive me, I prayed, because I just couldn't seem to wipe the taunting smile off my face that was beating the nerves right out of Parri.

"Jeena, I'm gonna let that pray for me stuff go because I'm not in the mood for you trying to turn my mood into something else, okay, before I really end up praying the hell out of you.

118

That's what's really wrong with you. It's not me, but it's your own can't see straight ass. You almost got your damn ass killed last year behind a married man, and then your stupid ass didn't tell Black about the letter. Now, you're suddenly feeling oh so bad about leading dumb Tanya down this road in the first place."

"Me?" My smile was gone.

"Yeah you. Sitting up there acting like he's all good. Look, I'm a Christian too...with habits I need to work on with my mouth, I know. But that's my only bad problem. Truth is, you should have told her the truth just like me instead of sopping up her tears and his mouth with a second chance. They're not married yet! It's what God has joined together, boo. It's not what God hasn't joined together let no man put asunder. That was the time to tell her the truth. Now, because of you, and only you, her throat is slit." She cocked her head to the side. "Now."

That was it. I broke. So much for me being hardcore. I was more like softcore as the tears started to pour from my tired eyes. At that particular point, I didn't want to stay anywhere around Parri because I'd realized that I wasn't really mad at her. I was mad at everything, and she was just the person with whom I could lash out.

Before I could open the bathroom door and leave, what I thought was an angry Parri, stopped me and gave me a huge hug. I could do nothing but lean back onto her and cry, and boy did I cry! A river was on Parri's shoulder, and there was about to be another storm on her other shoulder until we separated.

"Jeena, I'm sorry. No I'm not perfect, and you honestly don't know all the shit I get into because I handle it right then. I don't expect you and Tanya to be that way but at least know that I'm coming from a good place, a good, honest place. I refuse to be nice and lie. And you are right. I do need prayer because there has to be somewhere in the Bible where God talks about a mouth like mine!" she laughed. "I'm sorry for what I said, too, because even though I didn't like it when you didn't roll out with me against Tanya's decision, it's still her decision. It's not your fault that she's in the hospital today or any other day. I'm sorry. We still girls?" Parri asked as she put that squinted eye look on her face that irritated the heck out of me.

"Yeah, you my girl. I'm sorry, too. I just hate it when you're always right."

"Right about everyone else's life, sis, but I fail too many times on my own. What we need to do though is get out of this bathroom before we catch a case of the kudies. For the record though, I know you just needed to lash out because you're over stressed. Just don't do that shit again," she laughed. "That crap made no damn sense."

We left the bathroom, and no one was looking our way. As a matter of fact, no one was in the waiting area.

"She was gonna rob him, Parri."

She stopped cold in her tracks. "Steal from who?"

"Tony. She was gonna take all his money. I'm assuming something went wrong."

Parri's feet stopped moving, and she plopped into the seat that was right beside her. Then she glanced up at me and said, "Say what?"

"What did I say?" I asked rhetorically.

"So you mean..."

"Yeah, she could have potentially gotten herself caught up in much more than what we think. Just don't say anything because Tanya will eventually tell you when she comes out of

120

this." I took a seat beside her in a seat that felt like someone just got out of it. It was warm already.

"Oh my God…like for real. I'm not taking His name in vain."

"Yeah, well," I shrugged, looking in the direction of where Tanya's mom and the kids were sitting. "Wonder where they went?" I asked.

"I think they may have gone to grab a bite to eat or outside somewhere because that's what they were saying before I got up. Tanya's gonna be back there for a while so…"

As Parri spoke, Black came bolting from the elevator. I didn't stand up to get his attention at first, and Parri noticed. Instead of the being the know it all this time, I looked at her, but she held her tongue. Her battle mouth didn't even open, and to even more of my shock, she didn't have a know it all look on her face either. She was going to let me handle my marriage. I felt it.

When I finally stood up to wave Black my way, I thought about what Parri told me in the car. Would I tell him about that threatening note from the wedding or would I let it go? I didn't know. I just knew that Black was now headed my way, and time was up.

"Hey, baby girl."

It was so refreshing to see him and smell him as he reached around me to give me a gentle hug. His dreadlocks smelled good as usual, and he smelled like the shower he took after we made love before I left. I embraced him like I hadn't seen him in months, and he did the same to me.

"What's up, Parri," he stated, offering his hand to her. She accepted, standing up and giving him a hug. He was such a gentleman that he gave her a peck on the cheek in support of her as well because he knew that she was alone in this.

"What's up, Black? How are you?"

"I'm good," he said, tightening his grip on my hand. "I'm good. I'm gonna go talk to Jeena real fast."

"No, here. You can take my seat. I'm going to go find Faith and Tanya's mom. They should be somewhere around here."

"Yeah, I just saw them outside, right outside the lobby. You can't miss 'em."

"Thanks. See you two in a minute. Call me when you see the doctor, if he comes back out."

"Okay, Parri," I responded as she left me alone with whom I hoped wouldn't end up being the ex-love of my life. I could feel Black waiting on me to say something to him as the elevator closed behind Parri. My hand was cradled in between both of his as he held them in his lap. He was sitting back, legs apart with his arms rested on the arms of the seat. As far as myself, I was sitting up straight on the edge of the seat, far more tense than what I'd liked, but I didn't know how to calm down. There was so much I needed to say to Black but didn't know how to say it. There was also so much he needed to say to me, but he just simply wasn't. I was living a non-upfront nightmare!

"Black, are you cheating on me?" I was going to ask this question for the last time. He'd better answer me straight because if I found out otherwise, there would be hell to pay later.

He closed his eyes, took a deep breath and then sat up straight. With is soft brown eyes, he looked at me, and I melted inside because I knew when he was telling the truth…at least I thought I did…and this is what his eyes looked like. They looked like the truth without him even answering with his mouth.

"No. I never have, and I never will. Jeena, if I wanted someone else, I'd leave you. Simple as that. I'm a man, Jee. I know what I want. Little boys do that, and I don't need to save no other lady in the wing. I go for what I want, and I went for you. I don't cheat. I'm not the world's finest brother on the planet, but I can get a woman without having two, three or one on reserve. I'm a husband. Besides that, I'm your husband. I can't give away what doesn't belong to me because I don't just belong to myself anymore. I belong to you, too. Only you can give me away, baby, and I hope you don't." He pulled my other hand in onto his lap. "I'll get down to the bottom of it. I will." Then, he changed the subject. "Did you find out exactly what happened yet… to Tanya, I mean? Faith told me that she was still in surgery."

"No, but there's a bunch of serious mess I think she got tangled up in with her man Tony. I'm not sure about everything, but he was a drug trafficker. I also know for a fact that Tanya was planning on taking him for his money. She told me that earlier today. When I left the house, we got the call from her struggling, begging for help. We found her in the tub with her throat slit, blood everywhere…" I choked up.

"Shh…come here. It's alright." I laid my head on his shoulder as he caressed my hair. "I'm glad she's alive and the rest of you are as well. This is a messed up week. So much for the honeymoon, right?" he laughed in another one of his attempts to ease the tension of the night. "You wanna go back on one?"

"I wish we could go away, and then we could stay away for like three months," I smiled. Suddenly, I felt really weak and hungry at the same time, so I sat up and swallowed. "Black, will you run and get me a quick candy bar or something from the machine. I feel drained and for some reason, I'm super starved. I feel like my blood sugar…"

"Excitement probably just fooled your body. I got you, baby. Hold tight."

"Oh gosh!" I leaned way over, so far over that my hair nearly touched the floor.

"What?" Black stopped his gait and looked back, but it was already done. Beneath my feet and now spreading even further was a load of vomit, and I continued to gag.

Black ran back to my side, grabbing me from behind, trying to help me breathe, but each time I took a breath, I gagged. With each gag, not much more came out but traces of pink, basic bile, which was disgusting.

"Get up, Jeena, and let's go to the bathroom. I have to go get some help cleaning this up."

He helped me to the bathroom with my change of clothes, and I handed him a load of hand towels to spread across the mess while he went to get some gloves and a janitor to help him clean the globs of smelly grossness I left on the floor. What a mess I made!

"Man, ever since I ate that dang steak. Lynia," I groaned recalling the short time I spent dogging out the steak she cooked. "I just need a soda." I rinsed out my mouth and during the rinse, I heard a knock at the bathroom door.

"I brought you a toothbrush and paste that I got from the nurse, baby. You alright?"

I opened the door. "Thanks. Sorry about that. I don't know what happened...ever since I ate..."

"Hold up, baby. Let me go and get this for the lady over here. Be right back." He rushed over to the female janitor who was about to get on her hands and knees, but like the man he is, he offered his assistance, grabbed some extra gloves and got to work on my vomit before the whole waiting area smelled like rotten stomach.

As the bathroom door shut once again, my cell went off. It was Faith. "Yeah," I answered.

" You sound like you just woke up and ran a mile, Jeena."

"I just threw up all over the floor. Ever since I ate this steak my new tenant made, my stomach is rejecting everything."

"Are you pregnant?"

"No," I stated calmly. "Just because I'm no longer celibate doesn't mean that I'd be that lucky to get pregnant the very first time me and Black hooked up as husband and wife."

"Weirder things happen. Anyway, did the doctor come out yet?"

"No, but I'm about to go back out with Black. I'll call you when he does."

"Okay...better take a test." She hung up the phone.

Pregnant? I fell against the wall, not even caring that it was the bathroom wall. When I finally came to my senses though, I peeled my back off of the potentially disease ridden thing as I focused in on the possibility of being pregnant after just two weeks of the constant bump and grind with Black. Could it be, I asked myself?

Jumping back in front of the mirror, I lifted my shirt and turned to the side. I inhaled and then exhaled, stood up straight and then I humped over, but everything looked the exact same. I knew if I was with child that I wouldn't be able to see anything yet, but I only wanted to see if everything was really possible.

I started to feel nauseous again, and then it finally sank in. Faith was right. I needed to get to the bottom of this, and where there was a hospital, there was a nearby drugstore. I was going.

My teeth and tongue I brushed twice because the wack toothbrush they gave Black for me to use had to be the cheapest brush in the world. The bristles bent permanently on the first go round, so I spit rinsed and reloaded. This was terrible, but I had to do it. Next, I gathered all of the thoughts that were about to combust in my head before I left the restroom.

I wasn't going to tell Black about the pregnancy possibility. If I wasn't pregnant, then I wouldn't have led him on, getting him all excited about it. If I was pregnant, then the test would prove it, and we could move forward – hopefully. I believed Black about not cheating by about seventy percent because of my desire to believe him, but then again, there was that last thirty percent that I wasn't too sure about.

"Baby, you alright?"

"Yeah, yeah. I'm coming out now." I wiped the loose water from my lips, opened the door and looked Black straight in the eyes, all changed up in my new clothes.

"Black, I need to tell you something. It's something that I hadn't been straight with you about."

The look Black gave me was dang near divorce style. I knew what he was thinking – that I'd giving up my vahjayjay to the next man. Due to my past, that had to be exactly what he thought was about to come crawling out of my mouth. He was so wrong.

I took his hand and led him to the very back of the waiting area so that we could be overlooked if Parri or Faith came walking out of the elevator. As I sat down, I crossed my legs and faced him as he hesitantly took a seat.

"What is it?"

"I kinda hid something from you on our honeymoon." My neck quivered, and I cleared my throat to calm it down. I was shaking so badly, and I watched Black as he noticed every quiver in my fingers. Then, he looked away from my face and immediately sat his head into his hands, his dreads falling to cover his whole profile.

"Man, Jeena, please..."

"No, no, Black, just listen," I removed his hand from his head, and he then slouched back into the chair, his head cocked to the side. I knew he was dealing with a lot already, and this secret wasn't going to make it any better.

"That card in the limo, it wasn't a real congrats."

Black just sat there obviously awaiting the climax of what I had to reveal. His eyes were completely closed like he was focused on getting through it, no matter how bad it could've been. Therefore, I continued.

"It was the note that I picked up from the chair. When I opened it in the limo it was a threat. It said *congratulations but this shit ain't over*. I hid it from you because I thought that I didn't need to tell you about that after all you've done for me, and I just wanted us to be able to start all over fresh."

"You mean to tell me," he started with his eyes still shut, "that somebody threatened us on our wedding day?"

"Yeah, and I saw her walking away, but couldn't make her out. She was long gone by the time we got to the limo. I brushed it off because I thought it was a guest that just left early, until I actually opened the card."

"Jeena, why didn't you tell the cops?" he dragged.

"I told you I just..."

"You still got the card?" he said, jumping up with his hands out.

"Well, yeah, it's in the house in my personal drawer."

"Well, we'll take it to the cops this week! What the heck this man threatening you from the jailhouse for? He had a key to your spot, but mine, oh, I'm ready, baby. Stick and move, stick and move!" He started to dance around like a boxer. I was feeling better already. He wasn't mad, and I was glad that he wasn't even shaken up. I thought I even saw him grin.

"So you're really not mad that I didn't tell you?"

"Naw, baby, I'm glad you didn't tell me until now really because that would have messed up my mojo."

I kicked him in his leg, and he pretended that it hurt more than what it did. He was probably happy that it wasn't as bad as the things that were currently going on. That's when I spotted the elevator open and the crew fall back into place inside the waiting area. At the same time, the doctor came through the doors. Both myself and Black rushed over to congregate next to Tanya's mother, Parri, Faith and the kids. Before we even got there, we realized the tears flowing down her face and started to think the worst, but then we found out that the news on Tanya was just what we'd prayed for.

"Your daughter is going to be fine, ma'am. Right now, she's asleep, but soon, she'll be up and ready to move though in pain. We do ask that you don't make her feel like she has to talk as there was damage to her vocal chords and neck, but other than that, all the swelling should go down in a matter of days to weeks. Whoever cut her, tried to kill her, but thank God they didn't succeed."

"And I thank God that you were able to tend to her needs well, doctor. May God bless you and those working hands."

"Well, I'm a Christian as well as a doctor, and I always say that it takes God to get the sick person to me sometimes. After that, it takes God to lead me into the masterful maze of a body that he created. I'll be praying with you. Now, the children can't come back, however, Ms. Bell, you can come on back if you like with only two other people for only a few minutes. Remain quiet, please, in the room as not to disturb her just in case she starts to come out of the sedation."

The first hand Ms. Bell grabbed was mine. The second hand was Faith's, and then we all, moved into the room together. Parri and Black handled the children.

Walking back was a bit of a nightmare because we didn't know what she would look like. On the other hand, what we saw in the bathroom wasn't anything worth a cake and a smile either. All I knew was that I was happy that she made it and was still making it by the grace of our Lord and Savior Jesus Christ. It made me happy that we were all alive, and whatever differences we had could be fixed as long as we were living.

I made the decision to take full advantage of living my life to fix the broken parts of it when I saw Tanya's face. Immediately, upon entering the room, Faith ran by her side and fell down on her knees to pray. I followed suit, careful to only touch the sheets and not her as she rested. Prior to me joining in with Faith, I watched as Ms. Bell walked up to her child's face which was bandaged up, kissing it lightly. Then, she remained standing to pray, hands lifted directly above her daughter's head, and at the moment I closed my eyes, I felt the glory of the Lord in the room with us. I knew everything was alright, and that was why I ended my prayer with a thank you and Amen.

We left the hospital after getting Ms. Bell a nice meal to eat because she wasn't going anywhere. As a matter of fact, the nursing staff got her some blankets and pillow from the inventory so she could get as comfortable as she could until Tanya could be moved from intensive care.

Black drove back home after hauling the kids to the hotel behind me, Faith, and Parri. I had to abort my plans with the hotel, gather my things and leave. While there, Faith decided to join Parri at her house for a short while with Tanya's kids before she trekked back home. The kids would have stayed with me at my house, but Faith and Parri didn't want to curb more issues over on my already dire situation. They were well aware that although things were peachier with me and Black, worst could come later, so it would be better to leave the children out of the mix.

On the way back home, I slowed the car down at the light but didn't come to a complete stop. It was pitch black outside, and I was dead center the road checking my rear view mirrors. I didn't need any surprises jumping out from the darkness, but then, that's when I remembered. The dang pregnancy test that I was supposed to buy! I did a U-turn.

"And I just passed by the drug store. Dog!"

By the time I got to the drug store, it was officially twelve thirty in the morning, and by all accounts, I was beat down with sleepiness. Entering the drug store, I knew exactly where to go and what kind of pregnancy tests I wanted. Yep, I was going to take two. I knew that taking one this early may have had a big mishap going on, so two was going to solidify the urine's argument for yea or nay.

After speeding my feet along down the aisle, I made my way to the tests, picked them up, and headed to the pharmacy.

There she was – the pharmacist – and she was either high off the meds she was filling or she was asleep.

"Ma'am?" Her neck popped up as soon as she heard my voice.

"May I help you? So sorry. You weren't here long were you?"

"No, don't worry about it. I need to pay for these and run to the bathroom to use them."

She slid the pregnancy tests over the scanner and placed them in the bag. "Thirty two dollars…"

"Thirty who?"

"Thirty two dollars, ma'am. You chose what they say is the top of the line."

"Any cheaper?" I cut her off again.

"Well, not by much, but this brand says it can tell within two weeks. So how far along are you thinking you are?"

"About that long – two weeks. Just lemme have them." I rolled my eyes, paid for the most expensive piss sticks ever and walked like a troll to the bathroom. After the money I spent on absolutely nothing, I was hoping that I didn't waste my cash. On the other hand, I didn't want to be pregnant based off of the cash I spent either. Truthfully, I didn't know what I needed to be or feel. All I knew was that I was vomitose, and I had to stop.

The toilet. I was beginning to hate this place. Staring down at the pregnancy tests, I dreamed of more happy times with me and Black. I didn't want the results to be under a small, jet black cloud of what ifs and who done its in my head. There would have been nothing better than to take these pregnancy tests in all joy. In reality, my joy was slightly tainted with side eyes to my husband and one of my favorite girlfriends lying half dead in the hospital.

Opening the box felt like opening new life before the results even showed. I'd never taken one of these before, therefore, the directions were in full focus in front of my sleepy eyes.

"Tilt the stick and pee. The results will show right here…" I stated to myself as I matched up the directions with the stick. "Here goes nothing. Come on, Jeena, you wanted to be pregnant. Don't chicken out now."

And I flowed, having never stared so intently at my own urine in all my young life. I needed to drink more water because the color wasn't quite as clear as I'd liked it to be, but at least it didn't dye the stick orange.

"Alright," I said to myself as I remained squatted in position, waiting for the two minutes to pass. The toilet wasn't about to be sat on by my butt cheeks, so as I tired from squatting, I stood straight up until the result came through for the first test.

I dropped the stick. It was positive. In the biggest rush of my life while a huge smile lit up my face, I grabbed the other test just in case the first one was a freak accident looking for attention. Unfortunately, I couldn't pee anymore.

"Dang it!" I looked down at my vahjayjay disappointed, but then got ecstatic once again after digesting the fact that the first test came out positive. That was good enough for me until later. I yanked up my pants, grabbed the old test and wrapped it in a paper towel. Then, I high tailed it home to my husband and…

Soon To Be Father.

"Do I know this dude? Was he at the wedding with Tanya?"

I'd finally made it home and immediately jumped into the shower. While soaking myself with the rush of water dumping onto me, the visions of Tanya in her own tub near death weren't going anywhere easily. Everything around me was going haywire, but everything inside me was going so right. I was pregnant, really pregnant, and I hoped that Black was on the up and up so that this baby wouldn't have to enter into a war zone.

"No," I responded in an elevated voice so that he could hear me from the shower. "He wasn't at the wedding. As far as I knew, they weren't even together then. That was another secret that Tanya kept from me."

My glass of water was sitting on the bathroom counter. That was the refill. I was piling myself with water so that when I did take the second pregnancy test, so much urine got on it that it had to be right - at least, that was my philosphy. I shut the shower off and immediately drank the last glass of water after stepping out and drying off. There it was. I was pushed as ever to go to the bathroom, so I opened the pregnancy test, and while Black was running his mouth, I fed the stick. Waiting was like the end of the world. You knew it was coming, but the anticipation of it all was overwhelming. This type of anticipation was ruled by the unknown – even though I knew. I simply wanted to make sure.

The results slowly came in, and it was just as easy to read as the first. I checked the expiration date on the box, and I was well within the date. I was pregnant for sure, and mommy hood was officially on the schedule. Nine months from now, I needed a crib, clothes and a settled way of life with a year's worth of milk – free milk. I was going to breast feed.

I started to jump around in the bathroom like a rabbit until Black knocked on the bathroom door.

"Babe, what's up with you in there? Why you got the door locked?"

"Uhm...I'll be right out. I have to show you something!" I was about to explode through the roof and dance on that sucker butt naked I was so excited. "Calm down, Jeena," I whispered to myself. There was a small crack at the bottom of the bathroom door, big enough to fit the pregnancy test through. I decided to use it to tell Black. "Black, baby, will you look down? I need to give you something underneath the door."

"Why not just open the door? What kinda game is this you got going?" he asked half asleep.

"Come on, just do it!" I slid the test underneath the door while the grin on my face spread. I swear I looked like the Joker from Batman. When I saw the test getting pulled from underneath the door, I waited for about five seconds, and then opened. There I stood butt naked, hopping up and down on my tip toes while Black stood there with the test in hand, mouth opened as wide as I'd ever seen it before, and then...

"This is yours, right?"

I stopped hopping. "Yes, baby, yes! We're having a baby!"

"Oh snap! I'm about to be a daddy? You serious, Jeena?"

"Look! Look," I screamed, pointing at the test. "Does that look serious enough for you? But wait, I do have to go to the doctor's office, so wait until I make the appointment. Other than that, I took two tests, and they were both positive."

"And that's why you started getting sick?"

I put my hands on my naked hips and poked out my stomach. "I guess he's what did it!"

"What's up, baby!" Black leaned in overwhelmed with joy and kissed my stomach over and over again. Right then, I felt like the happiest woman on the face of the planet. We were about to be a new family all over again in less than a year.

We were asleep in each other's arms when we heard several knocks at the door. I woke up and glanced at the clock which read four o'clock, and immediately I became frantic because of Tanya being in the hospital. I grabbed my phone and nudged Black in the side at the same time. My phone had no messages or new calls on it, so whoever was at the door was a mystery to me.

"Black, somebody is at the door, and it's four o'clock in the morning," I whispered.

"What?"

The knocks started again, and Black got up out of the bed while I threw on my stretch pants and a wrinkled up shirt from out of the drawer. Black wiped his eyes, slid his pipe out of the drawer and walked to the door with his boxers on.

"Baby, a pipe? That's all? It's four o'clock in the morning." I ran into the kitchen behind him and his dragging feet to grab two knives. One for the first stab and the second for if the enemy got back up.

"Jeena," he stammered as I stood behind him with both knives, one in each hand.

"What?" I answered flustered and ready for war. I jumped as the person at the door knocked even harder than the previous knocks.

"Who is it?" Black yelled. Then the person answered, and I nearly freaked out.

"Please open the door, Black. Jeena, please. I'm bleeding out. I'm bleeding out, Black," the man called from outside the door.

"Is that Tony?" I asked stunned, causing me to grip my knives tighter.

"Tony?" After quickly looking out the peep hole, Black snatched open the door before I could even yell…

"Noooo!"

It was too late. Black and I watched Tony fall into the house bloody from the stomach down. I dropped one knife on the chair to run and grab the cleaning gloves from under the cabinet and threw them to Black.

"Put 'em on, put 'em on and shut the door!"

"What…he got something? This Tanya's man?" Black asked, shoving the rest of Tony's body inside with his foot and shutting the door behind him, being sure to lock it while leaving the lights off. Then he shoved the gloves on while I stepped back about five paces.

"I don't know what he has, but if he has something, I don't want you to get it because I'll get it, Black! Yes, yes! That's Tanya's man. Oh Jesus," I yelled nervously. I ran over to Black's ear, jumping over Tony who was about to die in our living room. "Didn't you hear what I told you about him earlier, and don't say it out loud." I whispered.

"I forgot. This happened so fast. What was I supposed to do?" he whispered back.

"Leave him outside, and call the cops."

"I need some help, Jeena. You the only one I know close by that worked in the hospital. I think I'm dying, Jeena. Please...I been out back for two hours 'til they left."

"Until who left?" I asked. I couldn't believe he was out back in the yard for so long dripping blood!

"Jeena!"

"No, Black! Hiding where was that you said? In our backyard until who left? Tony, you're about to get us killed for you coming up in here! Do you know where Tanya is?"

"Jeena, I need some help. No, Jeena, I don't know where she is."

"She got her throat slit! That's where! Laying up in the hospital, obviously behind some crap you got her into."

"Jeena, just go call the cops," Black stated.

"The cops? So whoever is looking for him can come back to us?"

"Do it, Jeena!"

"Black!" I didn't care what he said. I wasn't calling any cops, mops, or coffins to my house. Tony got himself in this mess, and I was about to put him back out of my house quickly before whoever was after him came running up through here slitting our throats.

"Look, man, I'm willing to help you, but you gotta tell me what's up," Black stated kneeling down near Tony who was panting for breath. "Call 'em, Jee! He's not gonna make it."

"Dang!" I stomped over to the home phone and started dialing 911. I was furious. "Getting us in this mess...should've never opened the door."

"And let a man die, Jeena!" Black yelled obviously pissed off. I didn't know he heard my comment. I just rolled my eyes because Black didn't understand. He didn't see Tanya's neck about to drop off her shoulders like I did. I bet Tony murdered that same somebody Tanya told me about, and that same somebody's family probably came back to get him. Period, point blank, and end of the discussion. I truly wasn't feeling this rescue attempt, and it had nothing to do with love. It had something to do with protecting the house, something Black wasn't doing too well at the moment.

"Yes, we need an ambulance," I said to the operator on the phone. I glared over at Black who glared back. I could've cared less. What I should've done was stayed at the hotel. My pregnancy high was gone, and now our house was turning into a criminal's shelter all while my girl Tanya was laying up in the hospital, blood all in her apartment with cop tape, all because of that man on *my* floor. Black wasn't thinking. This would put us in the dead center of the madness. Dead...really dead center. "There's a man bleeding. He knocked on the door, fell inside and now he's dying rather quickly it seems. He was probably shot or stabbed, maybe even two hours ago, because he said he was behind our home for two whole dang hours hiding."

I was pissed off. This wasn't the way an already stressful night was supposed to continue on into the sunrise.

"Jeena, get down! Get down, baby, get down!"

"Crap!" Shadows were moving at the blinds at the back window, and it was all thanks to the motion light from the man next door. As soon as I saw it come on, I hit the floor and shuffled behind the counter just in case. Black slid over next to me and placed his body over mine, finally in protective mode, leaving Tony back there to fend for himself. "You shouldn't have let him inside, baby." A tear started to fall, but I wiped it so that it wouldn't make me appear weak. I needed all the strength that I could get in case something went wrong, and that strength had to show outwardly to any nutcase I might have had to encounter breaking in this house.

There were some voices out back, so I quickly whispered it to the 911 operator on the phone, telling her to send the cops as well and fast. Then the craze asked me if I could identify the people out back. That was when I hung up and shut the ringer off. If they come, they come, I thought. Until and after then, I wanted to keep me and Black alive. Black and I could do better on our own because cops were always late. Even if they got here before the predators left, there would be some deadly shoot out making things worse on us. I wasn't having it.

"Black, Tony murdered somebody."

"What, Jeena?" His body immediately turned to face Tony as a full out threat despite the fact that he remained lying still on the floor. "You picked a fine time to tell me that. Forget the drugs...what type of killer you mean?"

I answered in complete whisper, "A first degree murderer, meaning he set out to kill someone, and that's what the heck he did. Top it off with the drugs, I don't know who is looking for him. Whoever is tracking him...baby, we shouldn't have called the cops, not from this house."

He glanced at me and got very silent. Then he looked back at Tony. "They're gonna find out he's inside if the cops get here too soon. I don't have a gun, babe."

He was thinking what I was thinking. We knew that Tony had to have one on him. If need be, we were gonna use it. Black started to make his move, but I stopped him.

"Not yet. Just wait. There's no reason to touch that gun yet. Let's just stay here and look just like we look, you in your boxers and me in this, without fingerprints on any gun. That keeps us proven innocent in this attempted murder. All it will mean though is that I'm gonna have to answer questions again pertaining to another crime scene," I sulked.

"Aw man, Jeena..." Black started, but I stopped him.

"Yeah, no, baby...I'm in it now. I'm in it. My name...in court...once again..." I just placed my head onto the floor and listened for anything unusual. I knew Black was sorry, but whether he opened the door or not, Tony was on our doorstep dying. That meant Black would be back in court, too, and in the middle of it with me. I grabbed his hand. "We're in it together again. It's our house. I'm sorry, too, and it's not your fault. It's my friend's man. Who knew he would stop here?"

"I got you, babe, and you, baby," he responded looking at our baby in my flat belly.

After that, there was just silence. We continued to guess if Tony was still breathing because we couldn't see his chest in the dark from where we were. We'd also decided not to place our bodies into the line of fire just in case, so Tony, Father forgive us, was on his own. The first lesson I learned in CPR class was see if the scene is safe before proceeding with help. The scene wasn't safe, so there was no sense in getting killed in the process.

"Shh!" I heard something at the kitchen's sliding door. "Crap, that's the handle, Black! Is it locked?"

"Yeah, yeah, be quiet. They can't get in. I got that hooked up. Do me a favor."

"What?"

"Stay put."

"What?" I exclaimed. At that, Black slid over to the side of the wall right next to the sliding door. He picked up the knife I dropped in the process, and after that, I already knew what he was doing. He was planning on getting whoever it was at the back door before they got us. If that door came open, there was about to be a war.

I glanced back at Tony lying on the floor. He wasn't moving, and I knew Black told me to do him that favor and stay put, but I needed to be his back up just in case. I went for it. Tony had to have a gun on him, so I was going to find it.

Just then, there was a knock at the front door, and I slammed my back up against the wall and then laid down as flat as a board.

"Police!"

I heard Black scramble up beside me, but neither he nor I said a word back to the so-called cop. We weren't that crazy, and plus, we had reason to believe that it could possibly be the bad guys. There were no lights flashing, and something just didn't sit well with us at all. In less than three minutes, our doubts about cops being at the door were all verified.

Black looked out of the window and saw two guys with black skullies pulled down so low that they were literally unrecognizable even with the bright light shining from the neighbors. Black looked at me and told me to run down the hall and lock myself in the bathroom.

"Come with me, Black!"

"No, these ain't no cops. He patted Tony down for a gun. "They must have seen my man's blood on the porch. Go on, Jeena," he ordered with a strong sound of panic in his voice as he couldn't find a gun on Tony at all. "Shoot! We gotta move. Let's go."

We left Tony at the door, and ran back into the bedroom, locked the door, and then, instead of the bathroom, we went to the window. Black checked it out first, jumped from the window, and then lifted me out. Behind the house were woods. There were nothing but woods, and that was where we ran. I'd never run so fast in my life, my thoughts flashing back to when Andre' was coming after me. I was reliving trying to escape that inevitable thing called death.

When we reached the trees, there went the first gunshots. Black snatched me up off the ground and shoved my body behind a tree, and then slid me down. He then covered me with is body as he looked back at the house. My face was up against his chest which was going up and down so fast that I had to back him up just a little bit because he left me no room to move.

He didn't look down as he moved his body back. Instead, Black just made sure that no one was coming our way. If they did, I knew that he would be willing to take the bullet again, but I didn't know if I could live through that once more. So I tapped him.

"Let's keep going further in. Just in case." I didn't hear anymore gunshots, so we both got up and walked further into the trees. Then we sat on the ground and waited.

"I don't know why he came to my house, sir. Me and my husband just got back from our honeymoon not too long ago, and the girl he was dating is my close friend." I began to sob as I spoke to the officer. "She's in the hospital tonight with her throat slit. Tony just showed up at our door, and then some men came..."

An officer came out of the house, bringing Black his pants since all he was wearing was boxers. Another officer came behind the first with sneakers.

"Listen, we're going to be here for a while. Walk us back through from the beginning to where you ran, and then, since you aren't immediate suspects, we'll allow you to crawl back through your window, get your things, and the crime scene will be cleaned up really soon. It's your own option if you want to stay somewhere else for the remainder of the night, maybe a hotel."

"No, officer. This is my house, and my stuff. I appreciate the fact that you are trying to protect and serve, but I shouldn't have to leave my house for anybody. We're staying here until this stuff is done. Who are they?"

"We don't know yet, sir. We shot one in the leg and the other one laid down on the ground in surrender, but they still won't talk." The officer looked at me, and I was still distraught. "Ma'am, thank you for the information you've given us, and we'll be in touch."

I just nodded my head, but everything about myself was in a shake my head mood. I'd been up all night, everything in my new home was being investigated, and I was feeling like eating. My whole body wanted food, and my blood sugar felt like it was dropping drastically.

"I need something to eat, Black. I'm not feeling too well."

"Alright, I'll be back." Black went up to the door, but was stopped by an officer. I ended up hearing Black tell them that I needed something to eat and that I was pregnant. They, then, opened a window on the other side of the house and let him in.

As I waited, I noticed a car sitting down the road. Normally there was no car there. Actually, the car must've gotten there not too long ago because as I stood out front, I could have sworn the road in front of that raggedy house was empty. No one lived there, so it was kind of weird.

Starting to feel uneasy about an unidentified car parked down the road, I walked over to an officer to report my not so cop-ish findings. No matter what, I was going to tell just in case there would be a return episode of madness. Before I was even able to tap the officer on the shoulder, the car's lights came on and started to drive, and for some reason, I was stuck, eyes stagnant in all the smog masking what was appearing to be a red, four door...no...two door. I wasn't the best at makes and models, therefore, I only noticed some lettering on the back of the windshield along with the fact that it was a female. She was staring right at me, and she didn't even flinch when I looked back. I could barely make her out, but I knew for a fact as the car rode by, it was a woman. All the issues I'd had with Black came right back.

Despite the fact that I looked like a trash dump, I wasn't in the mood for the drama. If it was the other woman, my tired, pregnant butt was prepared to drag her from the car, against the will of God I knew, and knock the fire out of her in front of the cops. What type of woman drove by your house and stared you down but a nosey broad or a guilty one – guilty of messing with someone else's man.

"Here, Jee."

It was Black, but I didn't even turn my head because I noticed brake lights when he stood beside me. Then as I walked toward the road, the car started to roll again.

"Jee," Black called. He'd brought me a milkshake. I snatched it from his hands, then my cell phone rang.

"What the heck was that, Jee?" Black asked.

"What?" I answered my cell, not caring who was on the other end nor was I thinking about Black either. All the innocence I'd placed back on Black disappeared because of an unexplainable woman once again.

"Jeena, it's Tanya. She's awake."

Black's cell phone started to ring at the same time I got the big news from Faith, but instead of responding to Faith, I watched Black not answer his phone. He was looking at me, and I back at him.

"Your phone is ringing." I swore if he didn't answer that phone, I was gonna toss the milkshake in his face and go to jail on a domestic dispute.

"I know that!" he exclaimed, confused about what was going on with me.

"I bet you do." I just walked away. As I did, I turned to the side and caught him looking at his phone, but he didn't answer. What a coincidence, I thought.

"Hello?" Faith yelled through the phone. "Did you hear me? Tanya woke up. Her mom called Parri to check on the kids and let them know, and she called me right afterwards.

"That's good, Faith. That's really good."

"Why do you sound like that?"

I sighed. "I haven't gotten any sleep, Faith. It's more than Tanya...the police are all at my house." I rolled my eyes and drank the milkshake down so fast that I caught a brain freeze.

"The police? Don't tell me you went crazy on Black."

"It has nothing to do with Black, Faith. Tony, Tanya's man, was bleeding on our front porch. Black let him in. Two men were trying to get in to get him, clued in by the blood from the front porch left by Tony. Now Tony is almost dead or dead in the ambulance headed up to the hospital with Tanya. The guys who shot him are on the way somewhere, too, because the cops shot and got them. Meanwhile..." I paused and took a deep breath. "I'm pregnant."

"Really, sis? I mean, everything you're saying is all going on right now, including you being pregnant?" Faith asked panting hard, not believing that all this drama was going on simultaneously.

"Oh, but I'm not finished. A woman just drove by staring me dead in my unwashed face, and as Black came outside, because that's where we've been - outside for the last hour, a phone call comes through on his cell phone. He didn't pick it up in my face, but when I glanced at the woman's car, it seemed to me that the woman in the car was doing the calling. No, I got no proof, but instinct is proof enough for a pregnant woman, right? So, now, I'm back to square one. I'm going back to court, maybe twice, and this time, Faith, it's because I'm about to give birth and have a divorce all at the same time while testifying on Tanya's behalf for two attempted murders by some mob of gangsters who know where me and my unborn baby live for now. Peachy, huh?"

Faith's mouth was muzzled. This was the absolute first time she didn't have a Word of scripture to guide me immediately. As she sat silently on the phone though, Faith finally retrieved one that fit the occasion.

"All things happen together for the good for those who love the Lord and are called according to His purpose. Fear no evil, Jeena. It may look bad, but fear no evil for He is with you. Stay in line with Him, and He will be on your side."

At the time she'd found that much needed Word to keep me on the straight and narrow, Black found his way over to my shoulder and tapped it, causing me to turn around. He was faced with the frustration that was melted into my face as I looked back into what I saw as his cheating face.

"Who's on your phone?"

"Faith." I answered. "Who was on yours?"

He held his phone up to my face. "I don't know."

I stared at his phone. The number had no identification on it. It was blocked, and I knew it was that woman. This was too coincidental. The only other alternative to the story was that the lone female driving by my house was with the others who tried to murder Tony. The only problem was that the cops had the car that belonged to the mob duo, and her bright red car just didn't fit the whole undercover killer type car. It was simply the other woman, and I could still smell her exhaust pipe from where I stood. She needed to get that oil changed, and she wanted my husband to do it.

"That's mighty convenient, Black. She decides to drive by while you go into the kitchen to make my milkshake, and then she calls you when you come back out."

"Who?"

"Her!" I pointed down the street, but then calmed down when the cops glanced my way. Black came up and gave me a hug to throw them off because he didn't want any other drama to happen in the midst of the stress.

"Baby, somebody is setting this up. There's some woman, yeah, but I don't know who, okay? I told you that, now chill. We're taking that note to the cops after we get some sleep, the note that you got at the wedding, because that's the only link we have to go on to tie this invisible stalking to Andre'."

"Are you trying to tell me that the lady at the wedding, the one that I believe just called your phone, is trying to torture me? That somehow and some way she's helping Andre' out while he sits in jail?"

"Gotta be, Jeena. That's all I can imagine."

"Why can't he just come at me then, Black? This foolishness you want me to believe about some crazy, psycho woman stalking you for Andre' is insane!"

"You love me. You love me, baby. That's why it makes sense. Hurting you directly won't hurt as much as hurting you through me." Black lifted my chin so that I would look him directly in the eyes. "I meant what I said to you a year ago, and that's still the same. I love you, Jeena. I've proved that even as your boyfriend. I'm your husband now. You got my baby, Jeena. No other woman on the face of this whole earth, even in heaven, has my baby but you. It'll stay that way. It is that way." He kissed me on my cheek, glanced back at the cops, and then, moved away from me. "What kind of car was it, Jee?"

"Red is all I know."

"No make?"

"No."

"I'll go let the cops know."

"Yeah," I said. At that, he was doing what he said he would do – getting down to the bottom of it. I'd forgotten that Faith was on the phone. "Hello?"

"It's not my business, but it is my business. I heard it all, sis, and I tell you to take your time on this one." I cut her off. I didn't need her to make up my mind. I needed to do it for myself because I was finished with the advice.

"I'll see you later on. I gotta go."

"Jeena."

"What?"

"Congratulations."

I'd forgotten my reason to be happy this morning. "Thanks, Faith. Pray for us."

"I always do. Come stay with me. You and Black need a break, and I have an extra room. I'm an hour away from the madness with a full fridge."

"Alright. We'll be there in forty. Black wanted to stay here after the full clean up, but I'll convince him to come. See ya." No matter what, Black was still my husband, and he protected me from day one. Whatever was going on, I had to have his back as well. The last thing we needed was to stay at home after shots fired. As he was speaking to the cop, I walked up. "We're staying at Faith's. I need you to come with me." That was when the cop started to ask me questions again, and the sun started to rise.

I Was Too Tired.

"They're moving her today," Tanya's mom revealed as I walked into the waiting room. It had been a full eight hours since I saw anyone or spoke to anyone about anything. When Black and I got to Faith's house, we crashed hard. There was no talking, no tumbling and best of all no drama. It was peaceful, and after being up all night long into the morning, we made the most of it. Faith's extra room became our den for sleep, and sleep we did. After waking up, we both left her house. I arrived at the hospital to check on Tanya, and Black went back home. "And congratulations, Jeena. Faith let me in on it earlier today. You're gonna be a mom!"

"Thank you, Ms. Bell. I appreciate that. I'm just hoping I carry my baby to term with all the mess going on in my life." I was about to become an open book.

"What drama? It can't be any worse than Tanya, that's for sure. That girl..." She shook her head. It appeared as if she hadn't been anywhere for the past forty eight hours, but she did look clean. Knowing her, she'd found a place to tidy up, getting what she needed from the hospital staff since she wasn't letting go of the key to her house so we could go inside and grab her some extras.

"Faith didn't tell you the rest, huh?"

"No, what?" Ms. Bell asked.

"It's Tony. He was nearly dead on my doorstep around four in the morning. The cops got the guys who did it, but I think it all ties in with Tanya."

"What? Oh Lord!" Ms. Bell's face turned south.

"I'm assuming they'll question her about who did it as soon as her rooms change if they hadn't already. The cops didn't get in contact with you yet?" I asked. It would seem like they would have.

"No, they didn't. They didn't tell me anything."

"They still might be keeping things separate until Tanya talks because everyone is in custody, right here in this hospital."

"You gotta be kidding me?"

"Nope." My cell phone rang. It was Black. "Hello?" There was no answer. "Hello? Black?" There was still no answer, and the phone hung up. I turned to Ms. Bell. "It was Black. He must've lost connection, so he'll call back. He left after grabbing me some breakfast so he could run into his workplace, update them on what happened and then go back to the house to do a second clean up over what the clean up crew did."

My phone rang again, and this time, I caught it on the first ring. "Black, what's wrong?" There was no answer. There was just silence, and then I heard music start in the background. "He must be calling me, and he doesn't even realize it." I simply hung up the phone, and didn't think twice. I would see him later.

In the meantime, I closed my eyes until Parri, along with all the kids, came up. They all rushed from the escalator minus the newborn who was still with one of Ms. Bell's close friends. I'd never seen Parri look such a solid mess since I'd known her. She was a complete wreck!

"Parri?" I scrambled over to her because she looked like she was three seconds from meeting the Maker her dang self.

"I'll never fault you again. Those are some hounds."

I started laughing and put my hands up to my lips in the shh position. "Don't let Ms. Bell hear you. What happened?"

"I can tell you that it won't happen again. My refrigerator is empty, and my living room is a complete wreck. If I had to keep those kids one more day, I would swear off ever finding a man, getting married, and I wouldn't ever think about getting knocked up for life."

"They didn't go to sleep last night?" I asked curious about what all went down.

"Oh yeah, they went to sleep," Parri explained as she watched them embrace their grandma, "but those jokers did all the damage during the daytime! I took another nap and woke up to a tornado after putting the oldest one in charge. So much for me thinking he was responsible after taking care of the kids when Tanya was getting her throat…"

"Parri! Shh!" I glanced back at Ms. Bell and then turned back to face her. "So you already know that Tanya's moving?"

"Yeah," she said removing her sunglasses.

"Do you also know that I'm pregnant?" I asked with a squint in my eyes.

"What!" Parri yelled at the very top of her lungs.

Everyone in the waiting area turned to face me as I held my bare stomach with a huge grin on my face. Needless to say, I was embarrassed, so I immediately, let my shirt fall and slapped Parri on the arm.

"Lemme see!" She snatched my shirt back up in the air, and I yanked my shirt from her paws.

"Girl, everybody's looking!" I cut my eyes to the side. "Look," I said under my breath.

"She's pregnant! My best friend is pregnant! I'm about to be a God mom!" Parri screamed, and the whole entire waiting area started to clap. If I was white, I would have been redder than paint, but luckily, I was brown and ducking underneath my long hair. After the crowd fell silent and the congrats ceased, I looked at Parri who was still grinning.

"My little boo-boo. Hey, boo boo!" Her head was right up next to my navel, so instead of ordering her off, I thumped the back of her head.

"Ouch, stupid," she laughed. "What did you thump me for?"

"Shut up, you know why," I laughed back. It was the first bit of comic relief I'd had since the storm started with Tanya, and I felt great for the moment...

Especially When I Saw Tanya.

There Tanya was, lying on the bed in her new room with a huge wrap around her neck. She was sleeping once again, but according to the doctor, not one major artery was split at all. Unfortunately, her internal injuries were horrid, from a bruised kidney and cracked ribs, but thanks to God, she was going to heal and make it.

Talking wasn't an option. She could speak, but we didn't let her. Instead, she wrote with a pen and pad that we'd propped up next to her. The first thing I said to her was that I loved her very much, and the second thing I told her was that I was pregnant. Tanya freaked, and I regretted telling her because I thought she would choke down the wrap around her throat and bust another rib all on her own. Her mom interceded though and placed her hand on Tanya's shoulder, reminding her to stay still.

153

Tanya then lifted one hand in the air, and I knew what she wanted – baby belly rub.

All of us decided to keep the news about Tony on the down low. I knew she didn't really love him, but although she wasn't in love with him, I figured she wasn't a kid of Satan and wanted him dead either. She would find out from the cops soon enough when they bring her mug shots to identify who it was that slit her throat and nearly beat her half to death.

I spent quite a while in the room with Tanya and the rest of the gang until I noticed I hadn't heard from Black ever since all those false alarms. He would generally call me at least twice before four o'clock, and it was odd that he hadn't tried to get me back on the line, especially since I'm pregnant, no matter what our differences were. I still knew him to check on me and I him.

"I hate to have to run out of here, ladies, but I think I have to go check on something at the house. I have some sort of strange feeling that something is odd over there."

"Do you want me to ride with you?" Parri asked.

I studied Parri's body language and noted that she was desperate to spend at least one minute away from what I used to call the creations of doom, gremlins of lava, and even night criers. I was talking about Tanya's children. They weren't so bad if you caught them on the right day or night. It was a roll the dice thing. Bad one day, good the next.

"Go ahead, darling. Faith said she was coming up after work, and we have enough money here to keep the kids full and a television to keep them quiet." Ms. Bell then rolled her eyes over all of them. "And if the television and food doesn't work then I have five fingers and a palm that will smack the devil out of them just fine." Then Tanya began to scribble something on the paper. When she held it up, it read OKAY! SNAP SNAP! We all laughed. I kissed Tanya, and left.

"Girl, I'm so tired of those hell bound…"

"They're not hell bound, so watch your mouth."

"Well, tell me how some little kids can make your life a living hell in less than twenty-four hours. I would have been about five seconds away from swearing off kids for the rest of my earthly life. Not saying that I said I even wanted any, but the fact is that those little craps will make you change your mind from a positive to a negative. And Tanya better have some food stamps ready because she's taking me shopping. Those dang kids ate me out of house and home."

All I did was smile and look down at my belly. The elevator sure was peaceful. The four walls that I was surrounded by allowed me to go mellow. I wanted to stop the elevator and just stay there for a minute, just me and my baby, along with Parri for a bit of comic relief. Then, the doors came open, and we both walked out into more chaos.

"I just can't catch a break!" I sighed.

"What the hell?" Parri concurred.

"Ladies, you both need to go back up the elevator and take another one down. We have an issue here. You can either jump across or take another elevator, and my advice is to take the other elevator."

"You think?" Parri blurted out at the cop who'd wrestled some guy to the floor who happened to be gawking up at us in handcuffs. The guy looked like a dang sumo wrestler, and he was blocking the entire elevator exit.

"Parri, hit the door close button because I can't jump over that big dude, not even if I was wearing a pair of Air Jordans."

"And we definitely don't need big boy in here with us." She hit the button. "We'll go up a floor and take the stairs. Oh shit, his hands!" Parri started to press the door open button repeatedly because the elevator doors were about to catch his fingers in between the floor and the door. The man was holding on!

"Parri, the dude is trying to pull himself on the elevator!"

"No the hell he isn't!" After realizing that she shouldn't be helping the dude out with keeping his fingers, she hit the door closed button and in front of the cop, started to crush his fingers with her foot until he let go. The elevator door went shut, and up we went to the second floor.

"I need a drink." I fell against the elevator wall.

"Too bad." She pointed to my stomach full of pint sized baby. "I'll drink it for you."

"I can deal with an orange juice."

"The wine will be mine."

The elevator doors came back open, and we dragged our feet to the stairs, hoping we could dodge all encounters of that suspect and the cops. The good thing was that we did, and to our cars we went.

"Are you coming back up here later on, Jeena?"

"Much later, so if you want to come with me..."

"I was about to say...thank you, girl. You need some company anyway since you're in the first stages of your pregnancy and all. So tell me about you and Black."

"I hadn't told you yet, have I?"

"No, what?"

"I didn't want to talk about it in the hospital, but me and Black stayed over at Faith's house because the cops were everywhere at ours."

"Stop lying!"

"Parri, look at my crusted eyeballs. I'm not lying."

"Why were the cops there?"

"It's a big story that has managed to pull me back into court. I can smell it. Tony," I swallowed, "Tanya's man, was shot or stabbed, hiding out in our backyard for two whole hours. Tanya doesn't know. Only me, you, Faith and Ms. Bell whom I told this morning. Anyway, Black let him inside the house, blood all over the front door and on the floor, and then two guys were outside our house looking for him to finish him off."

"Shut up!"

"No chile, I'ma keep talking! Then, me and Black bolt outside in pajamas, Black only in his boxers. About twenty seconds later or something like that, gunshots start coming. My guess is that the first shots came from the police to what I'm going to call the drug dealers, but who knows because I didn't see it. All of them are sitting in the same hospital with Tanya at this very moment I guess. At least I know Tony is."

Parri stopped in her tracks. "Don't get your ass in this car!"

I already knew Parri'd conjured up a not so bright idea. "What are you talking about?"

"How are you just gonna leave when the people who tried to murder Tanya are up in there?"

"What are we, or what am I, supposed to do about that? I was nearly killed, me and Black, if he didn't rush us both to the woods behind the house by the grace of God Almighty, and now you want me to go up in there and find the dudes?"

"Hell yeah!"

"How do you know it was them that tried to murder Tanya? What if it was some other goons?"

"Jeena, really? Stop making excuses. Who else was it?"

I sat inside the car against Parri's wishes and rolled down the window. "Well, it's still dumb because the cops won't let anyone near them anyway. Besides that, HIPAA, so get in."

"Shoot!" Parri hopped in and slammed the door.

"Why do you have to be so dramatic and in the mix all the time?"

"I like to fix shit."

"Stop cussing so much."

"Sorry. Pray for me," she responded with absolutely no conviction.

"I'ma pray for you alright - myself included - because you tend to rub off on me."

"Sometimes you need it, sis. Sometimes you need it, without the mouth and the drama chasing. I need some of you, too, so we make a good pair, even each other out."

I just grinned, and we left the hospital parking lot. No matter what we felt about each other, Parri was my girl, and I knew for a fact that through it all, she had my back no matter how insane it may seem.

"Here's the crazy part, Parri," I continued as I pulled up to the stop sign. "There was this red car that drove by, eyeing me down, as I stood there looking a fright about to alert the cops, and when Black came over with my milkshake, the car stopped. When I peered around, the woman who was driving pressed the gas and kept going down the street. Then, guess what happened?"

Parri was leaned over on the passenger's side door with a huge nasty smirk on her face and her arm resting on the ledge of the window. I already knew what she was thinking – the same thing I was thinking when it happened. Parri was more than likely ready to go spread a good hard fist across the female's face.

"That trick backed the car up and caught a beat down when she got out?" she asked.

"No. Black's phone rang," I said turning the corner. "He didn't pick it up either. I had to basically yell at him to do it, and when he did, he said it was a private number. He even showed it to me, so that left me thinking that he was telling the truth and that a psycho girl was setting him up..."

"Or they were setting you up," she interjected.

"True." I had to agree with that one. "Then he told the cops about the car that drove by." Even though I didn't have much to say about it, I heard every word Parri said in that complete sentence that contained the words setting me up. "He also told me that I was his only woman, and someone was obviously trying to set him up."

"This is some kind of weird, Jeena. I'm not gonna lie. Too much is going down around you."

"Karma."

"What?"

"I'm getting it all back. All that bad crap is coming back, Parri. I know this is why. Stuff like that happened in the Bible...look at Jezebel."

"Jezebel? Girl, shut up. Jezebel's ole raggedy, evil butt needed to get swallowed up by some dogs. You aren't Jezebel. You're a saved Jezebel! Big difference."

"Shut up, Parri, I'm serious! I made one mistake and my whole life has turned upside down since I got married. It's like the devil has been set loose to bring on the hell and torment."

"Jeena, this ain't hell. This is just life where crap happens that leads you into a piece of hell to let us all know that hell ain't where we want to go forever. Life teaches us to stay our butts up out of that pit if we hate this small stuff." She paused. "Now, will you do me a favor though, best friend of mine?" she asked with a huge sucker me in grin on her face. "Pull over into the grocery store parking lot, please, so I can get something?"

I did. I was hungry again anyway. Pregnancy wasn't a cake walk. It was more like a whole cake eat-a-thon, and I hated to see how hungry I was going to get later when my belly actually did show. The first empty park I saw, I drove into, and Parri started in on me.

"Look, there's nothing wrong with your life now. Jesus may have disapproved of your actions then, but you got yourself back on track. Now, you can't say why everything is happening, and I can't either. All I can tell you is to live and make it through it. I never told you this, but..." she stalled and started to twiddle those thumbs of hers. She was nervous.

"What?"

"It's you that have already encouraged me to be a better person. Back then, when you told me I was jealous. Chile, you were dead on! I had to look at myself, lonely and all that, living through you and Tanya's love for a man. Yeah, I want a relationship, but I'm terrified because either I will be in prison for attempting to kill him or he will end up dead with me on the run. I'm just not ready." She shrugged. "Until I'm ready, thank you for staying my girl, even though when you got married, I got jealous as hell although I was still happy for you."

"Ahhh, Parri," I leaned over and gave her a hug.

"Karma ain't got nothing on a made up mind to live right. Trust me, Jeena, I'm trying. Look, I even got my Bible!" She opened her purse and pulled out the New Testament.

"Stop!"

"Girl, Jesus be telling it! Karma ain't got nothing on me now!" She laughed. "All this to say that if He loves me still in my stank, He loves you, too. Just live through this stuff. It'll be okay. We can get better each second we go. At least that's as far as I can see right now – second by second."

I just stared. Who would've thought it would be Parri to kick some knowledge to me about Jesus in this way? To admit that she had issues that ran that deeply was a genuine testimony in more than one way for our friendship because I knew that she wouldn't dare admit that to anyone else.

"Don't tell that to anyone else or I'll fire you on the spot. I'm not playing. Don't need people taking me for a joke." she said hopping out of the car, leaving me nearly in tears. I knew that took a lot for her to say because Parri was just that type to be tough no matter what. A little bit worse than what she used to be, but obviously trying to do better. I guess my thrashing did work after all.

As soon as we entered the grocery store, Parri rushed to the seafood. That was one things she couldn't wait to grab – sushi. In the meantime, I got a phone call once again, and this time, I didn't recognize the number.

"Hello?" I answered, limping behind Parri. I'd hit my knee on the door coming inside, and it hurt something huge! I had to grab a cart just to hold myself up and fake the funk. "Hello?" I stated again, and just before I hung the phone up, a voice spoke.

"Jeena, don't hang up. I only have a little bit of time, but I didn't threaten you at all."

"Andre'?" My voice carried all the way over to Parri who had the sushi in her hand, but dropped it right on the floor in front of her feet. She came running. My eyes stayed on Parri because I didn't know what to do, so I yelled, "Why are you on my phone?"

"Listen, don't tell anyone, but an officer gave me word that someone contacted you on my behalf. I *never* contacted you on your wedding day, ever. This is the first time, Jeena. You gotta believe me. Don't set me up for this, now, I know I did wrong in the past, but I didn't..." He hung up the phone, and I was frozen. Parri snatched the phone from my fingers and glanced down at the number flashing.

"This isn't even a jailhouse number, Jee."

"That was his voice. That was him. He said he didn't do it."

"Do what?"

"Leave the letter. Some cop tipped him off. He didn't leave the letter, Parri, the one that I told you about that was left in the chair at the wedding. He said he didn't do it."

"Call that number back. He used a cell phone from the jail."

"No, no I'm not calling back. Let's just get what we need to get. He wasn't supposed to contact me, and this whole phone call really isn't his method of operation. Contacting me was a sign of desperation. He's trying to get out of jail, not stay in. I believe him, girl."

"You believe him? Really?" she asked, dropping her head.

I stopped cold in my tracks. "Yeah, Parri. Black mentioned the card to the cops, and he wanted to stop to the police station today, too. Maybe that's why he was trying to call me. I thought it was just accidental because he never spoke." I immediately called Black again, but got no answer. "Parri, Andre' said that some cop tipped him off to the report filed against him, but I don't want it to be against him and the real person is out here with us!"

"Again, the crap is starting to get too weird." She rolled her eyes up in the air and started whistling. "Let's just get the food and go. We can go straight back to your place and sort this out on a full stomach. " She started walking back to her dropped package of sushi on the floor. "I can't believe he called you, Jee. That's something to think about over even more wine. Too bad you can't drink, not to get drunk of course, but just to relax, geez. What a mess."

As she continued to talk to herself, thinking I was right behind her, I stood still. There was no way I could tell Black that Andre' called my phone and in the next breath tell him that I believed...

He Didn't Do It.

It was quiet between me and Parri all the way to my house. Parri was chewing on some trail mix and had already tossed a palm full of sushi in her mouth. Of course, I couldn't eat one drop of raw meat, so I stuck to the same bagged finger food as Parri.

The music was on full blast. I didn't want to talk, and Parri knew it. In the back of my mind, I was hoping that Black wasn't even home, that he'd lost his phone or something of that nature because I didn't want to deal with it right away. Shoving it under the rug wasn't the best option, and I didn't want that kind of guilt on my hands that would send someone to get punished for something he didn't do. Andre' was getting his pay back in jail, but it was for something he *did* do, not over an assumption. Even when I thought about the situation of Andre' calling and me taking his side, it seemed like I still cared for him which wasn't the case. To anyone else, it would have made me seem like a complete fool. I wasn't though. I just didn't want the wrong man going down for something he didn't do, even if he hurt me and Black. I just didn't know if Black would understand that. The truth was that if it wasn't Andre', the nutcase is on the loose, and that's who needs to go down for the threat.

As soon as I stopped the car at the light, I dialed Faith. I needed straight calm talk, and not incidental straight to the hip and break it talk for this situation. With Parri, I just didn't know what I would get. I was gonna tune Parri out because I knew she was going to chime in, and I was only intending to focus in on my little sister. She was going to know what to do.

"Faith, where are you?"

"I'm on my way to the hospital to go and be with Tanya. I hear she's moved already, so I'm going up to encourage her and the family through this. I want to still remain prayerful. How are you doing? Are you and Black okay, and the baby?"

"Well, yeah we're fine. I'm fine and Black, I don't know. I haven't spoken to him since we left your house. He tried to call I think, but we continue to get disconnected before hello. But sis, I need to tell you that Andre' called me." I glanced over at Parri, and she continued to stare out of her window. She heard me. I know she did, but she must have been practicing keeping her mouth closed. This was the second time she let me handle my own conversation.

"Andre' called you?" Faith's voice sounded like she'd heard a ghost. "For what reason did he think he could call you, Jeena?"

"He thought it was alright to call me because a cop tipped him off about the threatening wedding card I told you about."

"Back up, Jeena. I'm not understanding here."

"When Andre' called, he told me immediately that he didn't contact me. He just blurted it out because some cop told him that's what was going on. Faith, he said it wasn't him, and..." I looked over at Parri who still had her head gazing out of the window. "I believed him."

"Here we go," Parri finally interrupted letting out a big sigh. Then she looked up in the air, clenching her fists. "I'm trying, Lord, but she makes it so hard sometimes."

""What makes you believe him?" asked Faith. She had a way of dissecting things without being rude and over the top. This was what she was doing – about to dissect everything that came from my mouth.

"It was the way he sounded. I can't explain it, but he didn't sound like he sounds when he wants revenge. He sounded like a man in desperation. The call was fast, quick...like it came from a cell phone. I'm afraid to call it back."

"Jeena, if it wasn't him who left you the threat via some woman, then who was it? Maybe another ex?"

"Faith, I don't know. That's the problem. I don't know. There's absolutely no proof. They have Tina locked up reviewing her psychological state, you know, and I don't know how that works. I don't even know if she's going to get set free or not by the time she gains a pass for being forced to do it by Andre' which was the biggest lie on earth because you know she's pulling the abused wife card. The only thing I know for sure is that someone is gunning for us. Someone is gunning for me, and I need to make sure I know who it is before it's too late."

"If you don't feel that you know the truth, Jee..."

I cut her off. "I'll find it. I will, Faith, I'll find it."

The stare from Parri penetrated my cheek, and I didn't have to turn that way to feel the gaping hole it put through my face like a cavity on a bad tooth. I placed the phone on my lap so I could make a hard right turn, and I listened to Faith's breathing on the cell. I'd frightened her, and that was the last thing I wanted to do to the person that I was supposed to protect from harm.

"Faith, I'm going to handle it."

"Yeah, you better because I'm about five minutes away from moving in with you and Black. This isn't funny, and if somebody messes with you, then I have to have your back, Jeena. I've been praying for you all this time to see things much clearer than you have in the past, and God knows that it's time you have this answer for certain. We'll keep praying, sis. Did you tell mom?"

I slammed my hand on the stirring wheel. "No! No, Faith! How come when we get all deep and stuff you always have to go and bring up telling mom? No, I didn't tell mom. You know she would move in really...not just say she's gonna do it. I don't want to kill the only mom I have with a heart attack behind this threat that was right up underneath her nose. Geez, Faith, leave her and dad out of this. It isn't that serious yet, and don't go telling them about Tony either, dog!"

"I was just asking, Jeena!"

"I have to go. Faith, thank you though for listening, and don't go tell mom about anything! I'm forreal... no Andre', no nothing."

"I won't!" she stressed. "I love you, sis, and I'm going to call you or come by as soon as I can if I don't see you at the hospital later."

"Love you, too."

"She didn't know what to tell you, huh? I'm right here, Jeena. Just ask," Parri hummed.

"Well what, Parri, huh? Go ahead and spit it out because I knew you were about to pass wind or pass out just to get your three cents rolling," I responded frustrated and out of ideas.

"Call Black and tell him Andre' lit your phone up, and then tell him that Andre' said it was someone else. Period. Forget how that will make Black feel because honestly, all he can do is go fool on the phone. He can't reach you through the phone lines to slap the crap out of you for getting him in the mess in the first place so..." she laughed.

"Thanks a lot, Parri, for the sarcasm. It's really making my drive back home an easier one."

"I know. For real, Jee, nobody knows what to tell you to do without second guessing. You may need to buy a gun. Go with your gut."

"A gun?"

"Yep, a piece – off somebody legally in that thing called self defense. It doesn't matter because whoever threatened you, did so illegally, so all bets are off. You've already been attacked once, and you don't need anymore threats. Be prepared."

"Parri," I stated as a confused appearance spread like butter across my face, "Ain't nobody totting no gun around near me. Nobody. I can't trust myself with one, so I'm definitely not going to trust anyone else around me with one either."

"Well, you trust me."

"What?" Did she just say what I think she said?

"Heck yeah. In my purse pocket, and fits snuggly, too. The best thing about it is that you can't see it bulging, so it doesn't interfere with my outfits.   It's one of those little pieces, like a first date little pistol."

"For real?"

Parri's head went up and down. "Yeah! I live by myself, and I have a big mouth. Don't you think I need a friend that's capable, ready and ain't scared to fire? You and Tanya are some chickens, and Faith might forget to pray for me one night, thus, little Pop Off," she said patting her purse.

Oh my gosh, I thought. All this time I thought Parri was packing a cold one with her mouth. "A gun? How long have you been carrying a gun? Is it legal?"

"A long time, and yes, it is legal. My time is far too precious to spend it behind bars over illegally carrying. Pop Off is soley for those who plan on doing more damage than fighting or screaming at me." She then, turned back toward the windshield to face the pedestrians that were crossing the road.

"You're serious, aren't you?"

"Jeena, don't get me wrong. I'll tussle with anyone. Using this is a last resort, and a busted lip and bruised eye isn't enough to pull the trigger. It has to be life and death for me, like asleep and someone standing over you like Michael Myers in Halloween or something. I'm not some random shooter with no brain. I'm not that scared of anyone to shoot and think later. That's crazy."

"Do me a favor."

"What?" she asked calmly.

"Don't ever let me see it."

"It's pink."

"Parri!"

"Okay, but it's not one of those long range ones."

"Did you hear me?"

"Yes, mother."

"Gahhhhh!" I complained. "Everyone knows that the majority of the time it's a friend who is shot by the friend's gun."

"Who told you that?"

"Life, Parri," I exclaimed, overwhelmed by the fact that the little purse she has placed on the floor really has a pink firearm inside of it. Why pink? Instead of just thinking it, I asked.

"Why pink? They make pink guns?"

"Girl, yeah," she said with a big old cheese smile, adjusting herself in the seat. "And they also had other colors when I went to the shop to purchase it, but that pink was on the money, honey! Ouw!" she yelped.

Good grief! She sounded like a country hick! Lord only knew that those people who sold it to her didn't know to whom they gave a gun. I didn't even believe Parri's story. She stole that gun, or some felon gave it to her. There was no way possible that she passed a test to carry a weapon.

"So you passed a test or what to carry it?" I couldn't help it. I was curious, and the conversation wasn't going anywhere fast.

"Are you still on this pistol? It's a mini, Jeena, and yes, I have a license to carry which is always in my purse," she stressed. "Even when the kids came over last night, the gun was *locked* in my safe in my *locked* bedroom up high. I take no chances when visitors come over."

That was it. Case was closed. I didn't want to see it. As a matter of fact, Parri really didn't need a man until she could turn it down by many levels, or I knew she would blast, stash and run if the poor man played any games.

I finally pulled up to my house thinking that Black wasn't even at home, but to my surprise, the car was there, all spray painted down with B.I.T.C.H. A.S.S. looking like a rainbow's nightmare.

"Dang, Jeena, you never lied. Black's car looks like a made for television version of Breakin' and a colorful episode of Beat Street."

"Tell me about it," I moaned.

"How I missed that in the parking lot when he came to check on you had to have been a miracle. Somebody got that sucker on You-damn – Tube and making money right now. Matter of fact..." She scrambled into her purse to get her cell, and I slapped her hand back.

"No you don't, stupid!" I laughed. "You won't put my shame all on YouTube to make a dime...without giving me half!"

"That's what I'm talking about," she responded, ready to take a picture of the sprayed monster in the driveway. Parri's red light came on her cell phone as she started the video, creating a full out movie as she stepped out of the car and walked toward the flaming vehicle. I didn't stick around to notice what she was saying, but I knew when she was finished, the passive income from the video was going to come rolling in because that car was a hot piece of destruction.

As I heard Parri shout the words that were spray painted on the car into the microphone, I laughed again while opening the front door of the house. "Black, are you at home? I've been calling you for a good minute now, but you didn't pick up." I got no response, so I figured he must have been in the shower or on the toilet. Black was good for hitting that toilet, and using the toilet away from the house was only an option if it was an emergency. I learned that fact within six months of us dating and going out to different places. He would get this weird look on his face, and I knew then that he needed to drop a load and couldn't wait to get home. Sexy, it wasn't, but real it was. I had to appreciate him for that...kinda. At least I knew that I wasn't attracted to him for being fake. I knew what I was getting, which made what we were going through with all this other woman and cheating talk so difficult. I thought I knew what I was getting, and for the most part, I still did know what I had. It was just that other small percentage that didn't work well with me.

The crime scene investigation people did a good job clearing up the front door and the blood rubbed all over the entrance. I noticed a bullet hole, but oh well. As long as that blood and body were gone, I was at peace to go in and out of the house. I noticed, as I walked to the kitchen counter, that there were new locks for the door, so Black had to be here somewhere. He could have even been outside, but when I peeped out of the sliding doors, there was no Black.

"Parri is so stupid," I laughed, shaking my head as I watched her through the front blinds as she kneeled next to the spray painted wheels while she traced it with the cell phone. I didn't know what she was saying, but if I read her lips correctly, she was mouthing *"turnt up, turnt up!"* and pooching her lips all the way out to look like a fish. I just hoped Black wasn't gonna look outside before the finished product, or that whole passive income on YouTube would be a wrap.

The refrigerator was empty, well, maybe not so empty. There was just not much that I wanted to eat, but I had to eat something else other than trail mix because the pregnancy was placing me on starvation watch. I felt like I would fall malnourished at any moment. Because of my stomach take over, I took the salami out along with the tomatoes to make a double stacked sandwich. I was craving nothing but food, and I'd never wanted it more. The bread was atop the fridge, so I slid it down, placed it on the counter and got to work making my semi-meal.

"Black!" No answer. "He has got to be ignoring me...sleeping or something," I said to myself after thinking about how he really didn't get as much sleep as he was accustomed to while having to take care of all this other drama going on.

I put the knife down on the counter and decided to head back to the room to make sure he was okay. The sandwich looked so good, but I had to urinate anyway, so why not wash my hands now before the good eating. As I passed the window, Parri was done with the video it seemed, but she was busy being her normal self – nosey – as she continued to inspect the car with her mouth gaping open as if she didn't already have enough. When I looked away from the window and down the hallway, my eyes met a pistol aimed at my chest.

"Bring your ass down this hallway, and if you fuckin' scream, I'll kill his ass."

"Oh God!" I collapsed onto the hallway's wall causing one of Black's framed civil rights canvases to fall and crack on the floor. I started to scream out for Parri but caught myself as the words *kill his ass* echoed in my ears. "Please," I started to beg, but she quickly stopped me as if it would do no good. She had a wild look in her eyes, and that wild look was mangled with tears that ran through her mascara and drowned her cheeks like a bad storm.

"Shut the fuck up, Jeena," she sobbed. "Yeah, I knew it was you, and as soon as I saw that announcement in the paper, I was gonna do to you what you did to me." She used her empty hand to wipe her face, smearing the eyeliner all over her cheeks to the back of her face. "Do exactly what I said, and if you turn your back, I got nothing to lose that I hadn't already lost besides the bullet that'll be in your spine. Now walk," she ordered shakily. I obliged because at any second, both me and my unborn baby along with Black, could've been dead at any moment.

I started walking down the hallway slowly, past all the black power artwork Black adored, until I reached about four feet from the gun. My heart, mind and soul were busy in a conversation with God that I never thought I would have again since I was left in the room last year with Black as he laid their nearly dead on the floor. With the gun pointed at my chest, I looked her back in the eyes, and that was when I remembered that I knew her from somewhere. It was the woman from the restaurant – Black's ex-girlfriend.

"Don't fuckin' look at me! Move!" She kicked me in my thigh as I blocked my stomach from her foot's aim, and I stumbled back into the door knob and then the floor.

"Black!" I screamed as I saw blood pouring from the side of his head as he sat with a rope tied tightly around his neck that was connected to the chair. From there, my eyes followed the rope from the back of the chair to the bottom of the dresser. It was a complete freaking trap, making him so immobile that if he moved too much, he would hang himself. The legs of the chair were anchored into the floor. It was rigged so that he would hang himself! What type of psycho?

Black didn't have anything to say because there was no possible way that he could. There was a piece of masking tape across his lips with a cloth tied across his mouth. I didn't even want him to say anything. His eyes said it all, and it was an I'm sorry. That was when I looked over at his ex, and I wanted to beat her head backwards.

"Didn't I tell you this shit wasn't over, Black? Yeah, you thought I was lying didn't you?" she asked, slanting her gun towards him as he paid her no attention. All Black did was stare at me. He wasn't even flinching, almost like he didn't fear the gun at all.

It dawned on me like a ton of bricks. "You wrote the letter at the wedding?" I asked in a state of awakening.

"You damn right. Ask Black. I told him I would get him. Didn't I, baby? Yeah, I told you, so congratulations, bitches," she exclaimed aiming the gun at us both as I tried to move toward Black. "Stay your ass put." She then sat on our bed, and I flipping wanted to scream because the only woman that was ever supposed to be on that mattress was me! She was due for another beat down for that, too, I thought to myself as my mind ran ten miles a minute thinking of a way out. I was so sick of psycho women that I was really ready to beat one down for the old and the new. Tina first and now this clown named...what was her name?

"Why are you here?"

"He got me pregnant, Jeena! I was pregnant! I wanted us to have the baby, too, ya know? I wasn't the most perfect person, but our baby was. That was my only chance, Jeena. It was my only chance to have a baby."

What? I stared at Black, but he continued to look at me spaced out, like things were hopeless. Then I looked back at the crazy lady with the name I couldn't remember that was claiming a baby by Black. I didn' t want to die yet, so I took it easy. I couldn't let Black go through this again for me.

"I'm sorry for whatever happened to you. If I would have known you were pregnant, I would've never married him. I mean, he would need to be with the baby more than me, right?" I asked, stalling with bad psychology.

"I had to abort it. I aborted it because he left me, and I needed a family for my baby! Y'all plan on having any kids, Jeena, huh, because that wouldn't be fair to me, now would it?"

"How long ago was the pregnancy?" I asked as she became engulfed in her past experiences which made her eyes blur as she continued to wipe tears. I was going to attack the gun as she wiped her face, but when my instinct told me to go, I couldn't. Not for fear of my life, but my unborn child's, therefore, I stayed put and kept talking, taking her eyes' focus off of my stomach.

"Doesn't matter now, because if our baby had to go, then he has to go." She pointed the gun at Black's head, then she changed her mind and pointed it back at me. "Or better than that, I can take your life and leave him with the hurt that he caused me.

Oh yeah, he told me already. "I hope it's a girl, so you can stop trying to keep my bullet from entering that stomach by your chatter and questions because that's where the first one is going."

She wasted no time. The gun fired, but she missed because I'd already jumped across to the other side of the bed. This freaking craze actually missed, but I pissed right there in my pants. All my urine came out, soaking through my pants as I reached for the long pipe Black kept at the bed. I made up my mind in those seconds it took her to reach me that I was going to live fighting because I was too tired and too pissed for her shit. Forgive me, Lord, I thought, but she was the one who planted that pregnancy test in Black's car. She was the spray paint artist who doused his car with rainbow colors. Worst of all, she nearly destroyed my marriage and just shot at my damn baby! I didn't take that lightly. I was about to kill her, gun or no gun, but I wasn't going to clam up. I was going to die if I had to, but she was coming with me, and we would meet God together so He can tell us our story, future and fate.

I felt the pipe, and as I looked up at her turning to face me at the backside of the bed, she was holding the gun high in her hand like she was a freaking gangster. That was when I tightened the grip on Black's pipe like I was a flippin' thug myself, lifted and threw that sucker like a flying saucer right against her forehead. She never saw it coming. The gun went off, but I was already in the process of diving halfway underneath the bed, but the bad thing was that I was at her feet. I did the only thing I could do, and that was reach from underneath the bed before she gained her bearings from that big swat I gave her across her five head, grab her ankle and yank it so hard that she lost balance and the gun went off again.

"Help!" I screamed to get Parri's attention as I scrambled from underneath the bed to its other side, afraid to look back into the eye of what I thought would be the barrel of a gun staring back at me ready to unload. As I made my way out to the other side of the bed next to Black, I turned back ready to throw something else at the sicko, but that was when I saw Parri. She was standing at the door with her pink gun in hand, her mouth sealed shut and staring at the woman who I thought I just put down. In reality, it was Parri. She shot Black's ex girlfriend cold as ice. I'd only heard two gunshots. The second one must've been Parri's.

Parri wasn't moving. I rushed to stand up, then started unclamping the dang noose craze-o tied around Black's neck while taking the masking tape off of his mouth. My eyes continued to rotate toward Parri who wasn't moving an inch. She was frozen solid, just staring down on the woman she just shot.

"Parri?" I called, but she didn't answer right away. I saw her eyes flinch and then her arms move only a fraction until I called her again. "Parri, it's okay. Thank you," I said as I tossed the tape on the ground along with one end of the rope. Parri finally glanced back at me, but she was completely silent. "You saved my life," I panted, "And that's the girl..."

In the middle of my sentence as Parri was in a cautious glance up at me and Black, a gun went off again, and I screamed, falling over Black and onto the floor.

"Parri! Parri!" I yelled as I watched her body cave in and stumble out into the hallway while her pink gun dropped from her hand onto the bed. Leaping across the floor like a line backer, I landed on the bed, grabbed that pink pistol and shot Black's ex-girlfriend twice in the chest. Then, I shot a third time to make sure she was dead before I ran to Parri in the hallway. She was bleeding out from her stomach, and I knew it was bad...really bad...as I took off my shirt and stuffed it underneath her hand, helping her to press on her stomach as hard as possible. "Parri, you're gonna make it, sis, you're gonna make it. Keep breathing, okay, it's just a little wound, no big deal, right?"

I was breathing frantically, and I ran to grab Black's phone off the dresser to call emergency. "Hello, I need help right now. My friend's been shot in the stomach, and I have another woman in here dead, laying down on the floor. I'm trying to keep my friend alive, so you have to please hurry. I need some help, I need somebody to help me," I cried, not able to hold myself together any longer. In fear, I reached out and grabbed the gun once again from off the bed, thinking that she might not even be dead. Trauma ran through my veins making my hands quake, and the woman on emergency was talking about reviving the dead woman, some mess about checking a pulse. That was when I dropped the phone because that wasn't going to happen.

"Jeena, I'm sorry. I'm sorry," Black continued to cry as I yanked a drawer out from the dresser and dumped it to find my box cutter or pair of scissors. The box cutter fell out, and I quickly cut through the rope that held his hands together so he could finish the rest.

"Parri! Parri! I'm coming, sweetheart, I'm coming. Don't worry about anything," I spoke, entering the hallway once again. I pressed my body up against her side, pulling her against me as I watched Parri grin that same grin she would normally give me when she was about to be a know it all.

"I knew I shouldn't have looked over there at your big mouth," she laughed. "Keep your eyes on the target. That was my training, and look what happened. Is it big, Jeena?" she asked in reference to the bullet hole.

"No, Parri, it's small in comparison to that big mouth of yours," I kidded.

"Well, it should be no problem, right, Jeena? You can handle it," she paused. "I want you to hold my hand and pray for me, pray with me, please."

"Yes, uhm hmm, yes," I agreed, sniffling and placing my hand over hers as we prayed. Parri led.

"Father God, thank you for your mercy on me. I'm not nor have I ever been perfect, but please forgive me for all my imperfections. I've been shot, and if I die today, please save me before I go so I can live in a better place and don't have to feel this pain anymore. Amen. Jeena, it hurts so bad," she weeped, and I laid her head on my shoulder and continued to pray.

Parri was shaking. She shook all the while Black freed himself and ended up standing at the doorway with his cell phone up to his ear in shock. When he heard sirens, he rushed to the front door while I listened and felt Parri's heart stop. It stopped, and it wouldn't start back. I shook her violently, but her head just collapsed onto my lap, and I tried for a pulse at her neck again, but it wasn't pulsating.

"Black, she's not breathing!" Immediately, I laid Parri on the floor to start CPR. When I laid her on the floor, her eyes rolled up to the back of her head. "Oh, Jesus, please wake her up!" Blood ran all through my shirt that originated from her stomach as I placed my mouth onto hers and blew my breath into her mouth. I watched as her chest went up and down, then after the second breath, I started chest compressions. It didn't matter that the cops were coming through the door. I didn't look up nor did I stop my compressions and rescue breaths, not missing one mark from the way I was taught to give them. That was when I also heard the ambulance pull into the yard. As I gave the next rescue breaths, my eyes met up with a man who lowered himself to me, but unless he had equipment or was ready to take over my CPR, his best bet was to back up off me. This was my friend, my best friend, and she'd just saved my life.

"No sir. No, sir, this wasn't my mistress. I'd dated her a while back, and she came back to my house. Somehow she was already inside because I didn't even hear a door bust or anything while I was asleep."

I was listening to Black's story as they drove off with Parri in the back of the ambulance. This was the second load of violence at this street address, my home, and I started to hate it. As I looked at the grass, dirt and just the whole foundation of the house, I wanted an earthquake to swallow it whole. There was nothing good that had ever come from living here with Black as of yet, and there was no way I was going to continue living there with an outline on the floor and a sketch in my memory of Parri bleeding to death and Black's ex-girlfriend dead from my side of the bed.

"I told you that when I was asleep, she, whom I assumed was my wife at the time, was on my back in a straddled position when I opened my eyes, but she immediately put a blindfold on me," Black stated as he glanced at me standing beside him because I was very aware that he was uncomfortable talking about it while I was there. Was I going to move? Heck no. What was good for the cop was good enough for me, too. "I thought my wife," he explained, turning back to the officer, "was playing games as usual, so I let her massage me. I just laid there, but then she slid a rope around my neck, that was like jump rope thick. She did it during the massage, so I didn't feel the rope first until she pulled. When she did that, I jerked up but she yanked harder and warned me to stop moving or I would die by hanging or a gunshot."

"Did you recognize her voice?"

"At first no because like I said, I thought it was Jeena, and she wasn't talking. It wasn't until she put the gun to my back and told me to get on my knees. That was when she got off me and guided me to a chair. I was still blindfolded when I sat down.

When I sat down though, she started speaking more, and," Black tightened down on my hand, "I figured out who it was, blindfold still on."

"And who, at that point, did you think it was?"

" Milanje, my ex-girlfirend. We dated for about one year and some loose change, but we ended it. She said that she was pregnant with my baby during the exchange in the house, but revealed that she aborted it. She blamed me for it because I broke up with her, but never, officer, did I tell her to abort the child because I never knew she was ever pregnant until today."

"There wasn't any forced entry, so do you know how she possibly got into your place if you didn't let her in?"

"Yeah, she used to have a key. I took it back from her, as well as the key to my ride. She must have made copies because look at my car and there was a pregnancy test inside, not my wife's. It was in the passenger's side door."

I shook my head. Never in one million years…

"Did she ever exhibit signs that she was depressed any times that you know of?"

"No, but she did see me and Jeena at the restaurant… aww man," Black stated shaking his head. "That was the same day Jeena found the pregnancy test in my car, officer."

"Is this true?" The officer glanced my way.

"Yes sir," I explained. "It was there plain as day. I didn't see it on the way to the restaurant, but after we got home, it was in the passenger's side pocket."

Black then started, "And you see what happened to my car?"

"We'll need you down at the station..."

I just walked away. Forget all this, I thought. Milanje is dead, and I wasn't proud to say it, but I was glad. Crazy trick shot Parri and tried to kill me and Black after aborting...

Her And Black's Baby.

I was inside the hospital, the only one not near death out of all my close friends. The emergency room was packed, but I knew that Parri was taken back fast because she was already dying when the paramedics got there. I'd changed my clothes back at the house, wearing a white shirt with an empty silver cross because it was a reminder for me that Jesus got up off of that bad boy and was raised from the dead as my living Savior bringing about those miracles and blessings that heal all whenever and however.

"Everything is possible with you, Jesus. Everything." Nope, my sister Faith wasn't anywhere around yet, but I knew she would hear about what happened soon, either from myself, Black or someone else which was how the grapevine normally went. All I knew was that this time, I could control myself because Jesus was my strength in my weakness. Too much happened to me over the past year, and I was more calm than ever waiting on word about Parri.

Black came through the doors in a rush to find me, and I raised my hand up high from my seat. Instead of coming towards me, he waved me outside. Despite the fact that I didn't feel like going, I got up anyway, and once outside, Black was leaning up against the building staring straight up into the sky. Walking over to him, I felt like he should have known it wasn't me on top of him on the bed. It was almost like I was jealous of a dead woman who he got pregnant. I was envious because I thought I was special, carrying Black's first baby, but in reality, I wasn't. I was carrying his second, and from the look in his eyes back at the house, he was severely hurt by the fact she had an abortion. Sure, I knew it was selfish, but it was my truth as I thought about my own baby. I didn't want him to think of our baby as his second chance at fatherhood and wonder what his first would be like with that psycho chick.

On the flip side though, I was still in love with him, so I couldn't be so wrapped up in my own selfishness to not see his side of things. That was why, when I reached him, I did my best to not talk much, but really listen without a natural lean towards my take on things. This was the same man that I'd accused who was innocent. This was the same man that I fell in love with and that took a bullet for me. This was Stay Black, and just like his name insinuated to many, he kept it one hundred percent real with everything. I could count on that. His dad raised a good man.

I leaned on the wall next to him, and he didn't look at me immediately. Instead, he took a deep breath while putting his hands in his pockets. I swallowed and waited.

"I didn't know about the baby. I broke up with her like I told you at the restaurant because I thought she was a bit much, not balling with a full case of quarters. We dated for over a year, like a year and a half, and she never bothered with me after the break up, Jeena, up until we saw her at the restaurant." Black's eyes were completely shut, but he kept talking. "Milanje used to tell me that she loved me, but I didn't love her like a man should love a wife which was what she wanted to be to me. I was straight up with her, and didn't mess around on her or anything, so when I saw that her heart was too tangled, I let her go in a nice way. She called more after that, but I let her down easily, answering the phone less and less until she stopped. I never knew she was pregnant. Jeena, she told me in the house that she was about four months when she aborted it. By that time, we weren't talking at all. When we started in with each other, she was about eight months or more out of my life. I was single for that long. That's all I can say about her unless you want to know more, Jeena. I'm sorry I didn't figure it out."

I reached over, pulled his hand out of his pocket, and slid my fingers through his. At that point, I didn't care about the back story with him and Mirageface because he cared enough to remain straight up with me when I could see that he was traumatized. I was sure he didn't want anyone to die, not even her. Me on the other hand, forgive me, Lord, but I wasn't too sympathetic when she laid on that floor after nearly hanging my husband, shooting at me and then shooting Parri who they still had in surgery after Jesus gave her back a pulse.

"Don't tell me anymore. I'm the one who is sorry, Black, because instead of believing you, I second guessed, and I apologize for it."

"Look, you're supposed to ask. I just wish we had an idea before Parri got shot or Milanje."

I rolled my eyes, but Black didn't see me because he was looking ahead. Bump Milanje, I thought. Bye, boo!

"She really needed some help," he continued with no sympathy her way from me. She got all the help she needed with that shut down in the bedroom, I continued to think to myself. Black had that dating connection with her, but not me. I knew that if Black had a choice about it, he would've head locked her, snatched her weapon and simply called the cops after trying to get her mind right. That was too much work for someone who hog tied him to a chair.

"And baby, I'm so shaken up by the fact that she was about to shoot you and my baby. But I only leaned on the trust that God heard my prayers while I was sitting there. I couldn't even yell or tell you that I love you..." Black choked up while talking, and I rushed to comfort him.

"Tell me now. Tell me now. I'm right here, Black. Don't lose your mind over this, baby, just tell me now," I stated while placing his hand on my belly. "While we stand here, tell us that you love us, and that everything is going to be alright because we love you, too." Nothing else mattered to me. I was pushing all things aside to save our love that we vowed before God. I knew I wasn't perfect, but there were always steps that I could take toward it, and this was one – forgetting the drama.

Black looked down at me and then where I'd placed our hands, a tear fell onto his wrist to travel down between our fingers. "I love you, Jeena."

"Okay, now say it again and know that I love you, too. Until death do us part, I love you. I love us."

"I love you, too. I love us, all of us, and I pray to never place you two in harm's way ever again."

"You didn't, Black, and we're fine. Wipe your eyes."

"Yeah, I gotta man up, huh?" he joked, wiping his eyes and giving me a quick kiss on the lips. "I just thought she was gonna kill the mother of my unborn baby and my baby in front of me. I couldn't move, Jeena."

"The point is that you are moving now, and we'll move forward from now because of God. Let's pray for Parri."

My phone rang, and it was Faith. I knew without looking because after all the drama, I'd set a specific ring tone to her call.

The ringtone was my voice saying *it's prayer time* repetitively. "Hello?"

"Tanya's talking! She isn't supposed to be but she's talking! She said hi, but shut her mouth quickly, and you know we're not telling the doctor because she probably hurt her throat pretty bad doing it because she started writing on that pad she had again and..."

I hated to cut off Faith in her excitement, and I was happy for Tanya, however... "Parri got shot and is in surgery now, Faith."

"What? Wait a minute, what?"

"She was shot, and she died on me, Faith, in the house. She's alive now, but it's touch and go. She shot the lady who was threatening me and Black."

"What!"

"Yeah, she was pointing the gun at me when Parri came and shot her point blank in the back."

"Pointing the gun at you! Jeena! What? Well, how did Parri get shot? Oh Jesus! Are you okay?" she asked frantically.

I remembered what Parri told me as she laid there bloody and fighting for her life. "She took her eyes off the target. When she did that, the lady shot her. That's when I leaped for the gun and shot her twice or three times while she was on the floor, killing her. When the cops questioned me, they got it as self defense. She had Black tied up in ropes, even around his neck."

"Sis, where are you?" she asked. I could tell that she was about to freak out.

"Downstairs in emergency until they move Parri. I already called her mom. Parri had her number labeled as mom in her cell, thank goodness. She's on the next flight out."

"I'm coming."

"Okay, bye."

My eyes met Black's, and we both walked back inside the hospital. We walked up to the counter to find out more about Parri because no one was coming out telling us anything extra. From there we found out that she was in the process of being moved to ICU to surgery, but no other information was given. All we knew was that she had to be critical because she'd already died once, and we didn't want her to die again.

We saw Faith come running, and she gave us both a hug. "God is good. He is so good, no matter what. Thank you, Jesus, for keeping my family alive." Addressing Black, she asked, "Was she stalking you?"

"Obviously, but it wasn't until she saw me getting married in the paper. She must have snapped. I made the mistake and told her to not shoot me because I was getting ready to be a father. She was going to shoot me, but then she decided to wait for Jeena to get home."

"It's all good now. I just thank God for allowing the truth to come out," Faith responded.

"Well, Parri is in ICU now, so we need to go back to the floor where Tanya started and start prayer."

That was what we did. Through it all, we leaned on the faith that we had in Christ, to be with Parri and Tanya, even Tony, so that there would be no loss of life, so that no mothers had to go through the heartache of losing a child. It was time to place all our faith in the One God that we knew saw all things. We left God in control and wanted a breakthrough for everyone spiritually first and then physically if it was God's will for them to live.

By the time Parri's mom got to the hospital, she found out that Parri had a ruptured vessel that the doctors were able to mend. The bullet tore through her skin and instead of going directly out, it damaged two organs. She was on life support, but the reason they said they put her on life support was to give her organs a chance to heal through rest. Doctors said it would be a fifty percent chance if she pulled completely through. We knew God said a one hundred percent chance, so we paid no attention to the doctor at that point because Parri was going to live. We were already thanking God for what He did in the future. When she woke up, we would be right there for her.

Everyone, except Ms. Bell and her grandkids, were in a huddle around Parri's mom who was about to have a fit because she couldn't see her daughter. I gave her the run down about three times about what happened, and even she didn't know that Parri carried a pink pistol. I didn't feel so out of the loop though because I quickly realized that Parri wasn't that close to her mom anymore. I wasn't certain why, but she knew nothing about Parri at all. It was like we were talking about two different people.

By nightfall, we all decided to stay up at the hospital and sleep, coming to common ground on the notion that it was the safest place for everyone. The next day, everyone went home to change and take a break while me and Black went to see Tony. It was definitely my idea because no one knew if he was dead or still alive.

"Tanya wrote his last name down for me, Black. I need to check on him, just to see if he can open his mouth and tell me what happened. Tanya told me on paper that she didn't know who the guys who attacked her, so I'm going to ask him, if he's alive."

"When you finally told Tanya about Tony getting shot, what did she say?"

"She wrote a smiley face on the piece of paper with the word GOOD underneath it in all caps."

"You serious?"

"Yeah. Dead serious."

"Wrong choice of words."

"My bad. Hi," I spoke to a nurse. "Antonio Daves please? He was admitted the other night."

"I'm sorry, ma'am. He's deceased. They took his body down this morning to the morgue. Are you his family? We haven't been able to contact anyone that is next of kin."

Stunned by his death, I responded in a slight stutter," No, uh, no...uhm but thank you." I stared back at Black, and he had a blank look on his face as we turned and walked away from the counter, headed back to Tanya's room to deliver the news.

"Should we tell her?"

"Did you see that big ole smiley face you told me she showed you when she found out that he got shot?"

"Yep," I sighed.

"Well, I doubt she's gonna go into an emotional fit over him being ice cold in the morgue either. Just tell her."

Black had a valid point, and that was why when we got back into her room, we spilled the beans. Tanya was resting, and the nurse was just leaving.

"Hey, girl," I hummed coming inside. Black stayed by the door.

She wrote the word *hey* back on the paper.

"Tony's dead, Tanya. I'm so sorry. They took him to the morgue this morning," I told her while reaching for her hand, but instead of taking my hand, she lifted her pen and paper to start writing. I examined her face, and just like Black said, not a centimeter of sadness consumed it. She raised the paper, and it read – *Go get the money, and how is Parri?*

"Parri is on ICU, and no one can go back there. Did you not hear what I said? Tony, your man and father of your youngest, is dead."

Tanya's eyes rolled all the way up, like she was having a slow seizure, and then she brought them back down. If I wasn't mistaken, I was getting on her last nerves talking about Tony and his demise. Tanya grabbed her pen again, started writing, lifted up the sheet of paper, and I read the words – *My kids and I need that money. His child needs the money. Go get it. I know where it is. The four guys who came in my apartment came to get that same money, but they only found one bag. Tony's dead, and to them, I am, too, and that means that those goons are headed back to wherever they're from. Tear this up... The other bags are inside his abandoned house he inherited, behind the master bed inside the wall. Tear this up and put it in different trash cans. I need the money, Jeena. If I don't get it, no one will because nobody else knows where it is but me, and well...you. I really need this money, Jeena. Please, and if you can, do it tonight.*

"Man, no, Tanya!" It didn't matter about my rejection of her suggestion. She still wrote the address of his abandoned house on a small sheet of paper and then put that *she knows I'm good for it* in parenthesis. Black was about ten paces behind my left shoulder, and I could see the tap of his foot from the periphery of my left eye. Since he was so occupied with his feet, I slipped the address from Tanya and shoved it in my front right pocket. Black was going to shoot me if he knew I was seriously...

Considering Tanya's Request.

I hadn't learned my lesson yet. There I was with absolutely no one to call on for advice about the matter, so I was in it alone. Faith was a no go, and Parri was fighting for her life. Tanya did need the money, and her kids would be taken care of for a long while with a load of cash stemming from Tony's bad deeds.

After giving me the address to Tony's inherited property, she also wrote down the fact that there were supposed to be two bags of money there. Technically, I wasn't stealing because I was going to get something that criminals wanted back. At least, that was the rationale I was giving myself as I walked hand in hand with Black back to the car after speaking to Parri's mom on the intensive care unit. Parri wasn't allowed to be seen for a whole twenty four hours, but the doctor was going to allow her mom back to glance at her. Although Parri would make it, however, there would possibly be some sort of brain damage done. The doctor said that he couldn't be certain where and how, but the injuries and the loss of oxygen posed a problem for her. Either way, I was glad God spared her, and a huge weight was off my shoulders as we walked back to the car. Black allowed Parri's mom to hold my car to save her money on a taxi and rental while we drove the B.I.T.C.H. A.S.S. car back home together all smiles, spray painted down and all.

We were totally inseparable, just like old times. On the ride back home, I didn't even want to think about Tanya's little run she was having me do to secure her hospital bills, kids' college and more, but I had to think about it. She'd given me the key to the place, so I wouldn't have to break in. She also reaffirmed that it was really her money anyway, left back for the family. I just sucked it in, wondering how on earth I would get over there to get it quickly and alone at night without a great excuse for Black.

Maybe Black would go with me, I thought for a millisecond as I caressed his leg while he drove. Then I thought that I would really have to give him some good loving before he swallowed this favor for Tanya whole. I would have to put it down like I didn't know how to, so I would have to try some extra moves. Thus, I quickly changed my mind because I didn't have time for that. Then, the thought hit me - just ask him to drive somewhere, and when we got there, it would be too late to turn around. I would feel better with him there than without him.

"Hey, baby?"

"Yeah, Jee?"

"Will you stop me off somewhere real quick. It'll take like five minutes. It's someone's house for Tanya." I couldn't believe I said it, and he actually said...

"Yeah."

...with no questions asked. I'd taken my shoes off inside the car but quickly slid them back on. Oh crap, I thought, as I felt a serious panic attack coming on, so I held on to the car door handle and flipped on the music so that Black wouldn't hear me breathing. I turned it up fairly loudly so that I could suck in air heavily and undetected. Then, I began to pray.

"Make a left at the light, baby," I requested like a sweet, little doll baby when in fact I felt like a possessed, evil elf. Tanya wrote down the address, and I knew the neighborhood fairly well. There was only one Pindale Street in the area, and according to what Tanya wrote, it was the house on the corner that looked like one million bucks on the front, but hell on the sides and the back. It was like the people who owned it, now known to be Tony, wanted to fake out the people who drove by, only taking care of the front – no weeds, fresh paint and all that. Too bad Tony didn't have brains enough to do the whole outside because the paint didn't even match, there was mold growing up and around the house and I couldn't leave out the fact that it was the biggest eye sore on the street. I was shocked it wasn't demolished.

"Where are you taking me? I know not to Creek's End over here," he said, making the turn and heading down the street. The neighborhood's sign shone like a halogen light it was so bright, and as always, there was the house, sitting on a foundation that looked as out of place and homely as ever. Just by appearance, absolutely no one would think or believe a guy like Tony owned this house. I was just as shocked about it myself. The house was dressed to make you imagine an old lady with moth balls and old minks with leather furniture and a plastic roll over the carpet with a scent that stood out before you hit the front door. It didn't ring out thug, drug dealer or probation officer.

"Yep, go ahead and turn in, baby, and it's the house with the nice front and bad back."

"House number triple nine?"

"Turn it upside down, and it will read the devil's number."

"Who does she know that lives here? I don't mean to shade it out because I know that's your friend, but dang," he stressed, "The house is messed up, Jee."

"Tell me about it." What was even more messed up is how I was concealing what I was gonna grab out of the house. Black wasn't a dummy, but I sure was acting like he came straight out of the womb on yesterday.

When we pulled up to the house, Black eased in to the driveway. We looked around, and the house definitely looked abandoned from the side. There were weeds growing up to about two feet high, and the sound of the crickets made you want to scream. I was sure there were snakes around the bushes - had to be -waiting for my ankles so they could sink their fangs in.

I was scared. I glanced at Black, and then he looked at me like *what*? The words *come with me* were on the tip of my tongue, so I asked, "Aren't you coming?" Well, I sort of asked without the full story along with it.

"If you want me to," he answered and immediately opened his door, headed to the front door, but just then, at that moment, I had to tell him. I had to tell him so that he could be on guard just in case something bad happened. Therefore, I rushed to the door along with Black in hand while he watched me like I was gone loco, and then I pulled out the key.

"Wait, you have a key to this spot? Nobody's in here?"

"Yeah, I have the key. Tanya gave it to me because she said she had some money in here, over in the master bedroom, that I have to get for her to keep for her kids in case something happens to her."

"Hold up," he snatched my arm back, and I checked over his shoulder while he did it because we were both halfway in and halfway out of the shack slash house slash piece of rubble. I was paranoid, and finally, I allowed Black to notice how shaken up I was.

"Black, there's some money in here that she said...well she wrote...that was left to Tony, or that was Tony's and..."

"Jeena!"

"What!" I shrieked, shaking my hands in the air. "Black, come on. Tanya will be broke without it, and she has to raise those kids, pay those bills, and how will she do it without the money, huh?"

Black just stood there fuming.

"What? You want her to be at our house all the time, begging for my interior decorating money? And what about money for her kids while she's in the hospital and her bills?" I asked.

"Jeena, I'm not stupid. Don't try and rationalize this drug crap she's in! Where is it? Dang!" He hit the door, and the thing fell off the hinges. I caught it on the edge, and Black shoved it back onto the hinges as well as he could. "A key? A key, Jeena?" I looked down at the key to the house in my hand, then back up at Black. He then ordered me inside. "Jeena, just go." I just stood there feeling guilty as a mug, but I guess I stood there too long because Black said it again. "Go! She could have gotten this crap herself."

We were in, and as we walked deeper into the house, it smelled like the master plan of funk. If someone or some animal was dead inside here, I didn't want to lay eyes on it. I just wanted to get the money and go.

"It's in the master bedroom."

"So the biggest room," he complained.

"Yeah, behind the bed and inside the wall."

"This has got to be stolen money, Jee, isn't it?"

"I don't know! I know it was earned, the dishonest way maybe, but it was earned with Tony's life, and Tanya needs it for his seed and everyone else's seed, too. She already planned on it, and don't you think technically that it's already hers!"

"This is stealing, man, and I ain't no thief."

I stopped when we got to the master bedroom. "How? I have a key! Tony is dead. It was his money, and by the way, this house is his inheritance, so we are here legally by his common law wife!" Oh crap. I said too much.

"You mean some of those gangstas out there could easily come in here if they know this was Tony's other spot?"

"No way, Black. Tanya assured me things were completely safe. Let's just get it and go" I responded, only *sounding* sure of myself when in reality, I didn't want to be there any more than Black getting the family money at all.

Black walked over to the bed, not ready to rationalize with me when death could be around the corner yet again. "You ready?"

I rushed to the other end. "Yeah, I'm ready."

"Well on three...one, two, three." We both pushed and a big sheet of construction paper covered the wall from where we moved the bed. "What kinda..."

I just shook my head, walked up to it and removed the tape. I could have easily busted through it with a pinky, but dang that! I needed to peek first. When I did, I saw the two bags Tanya was talking about. Money was hanging from one of the bags. Black rushed to reach in and grab them both as I stood back.

Black's car lights still hadn't gone off, and the light shined into the bedroom. The master bedroom wasn't bad off in appearance. There wasn't any dust nor were there any visible signs of rotted out wood or leaks as in the living area. It seemed visited quite often, just this room.

"Jeena, snap out of it. Let's go. This isn't a tour, and Tanya, after this, isn't your friend."

"What?"

"Come on, Jeena," he stated.

"You can't tell me who to keep as friends, Black," I stated, stepping behind him closely until he turned around.

"And why not? Jeena, look at me!" He shoved the bags of money in my face. "Do you see this? Look! This isn't the life I want, and I hope it's not the life you want because you can move in with her."

"Black!" I couldn't believe he said that!

"You got me doing this crap for some woman who is in too deep! I'm not her pick up person for this drug money, and you aren't either. Futhermore, she's not my wife. You are! If I would've known about this ahead of time, your girl would have been some thousands short. My job is to protect you first and nobody else but that baby in your belly!" He then looked outside. "You think people can't recognize that car? Did you see it because last time I checked, it had bitch ass written on it, and right now, that's how I feel. Got me cussin'..." he stated, storming out of the house. I rushed to close the front door behind me the best way I could and then tried to lock it. By the time I finished, Black was already inside the car. I was still speechless.

Despite the rant from Black, I ran to the car and jumped in, catching a visual of the bags in the backseat. They were so full that the bags looked like they would rip apart the next time Black moved them. Black's face was stone. There was no expression whatsoever, and I knew that we weren't in the same good space that we were at the hospital, holding hands and encouraging each other. Instead, Black probably wanted to burn the money and shove me in a ditch somewhere with divorce documents.

"Black," I started. "This is the last time..."

"The last time?" he yelled, backing out of the driveway. "The last time shouldn't have even been this time, Jeena. Now, where are we taking this money? I suggest you call Tanya, Tanya's mom, or somebody and tell them it's not at our house. I did this for you and your girl just once, but I'm not carrying some felony burden around with me in bags. You can, but I'm not. Friendship ain't getting each other killed, Jeena. We are ride or die, not them. They aren't in the equation."

As he spoke and before I apologized because he was right, I saw car lights coming down the road. "Black, hurry and straighten the car up and move. A car is coming."

Black did what I asked. I had a super bad feeling come over me that this was bad news. For the most part, this section of the street didn't have many cars going up and down because either the elderly were living here, or there were people who didn't own cars. The neighborhood was just that old, and the fact that I saw what looked like SUV headlights coming down the road didn't help my anxiety level at all. My nerves suddenly took a leap over the edge.

"Just look straight ahead, baby, and act normal although nothing is normal about this for us."

"Of all the times I've come down here...an SUV?" I panicked.

"Shh..."

We drove cautiously, going the speed limit just in case it was a cop, and the speed limit was only twenty-five miles an hour. How slow was that! It seemed like an eternity before our car met what I correctly identified as an SUV. It was driving slower than we were, and it was obvious that they were in search of something by the way they were flicking their lights at every mailbox. That meant that they had no idea where they were. They were strangers.

"It's them, baby. Gotta be," Black assumed.

"Tanya told me that they didn't know..." My voice began shaking.

"Now ain't the time to start crying, Jee. Wipe your eyes and put your head on my shoulder like you're asleep. Knock those bags down on the floor when you do it. Hurry up. We need to get to the end of the road before they even get in the house."

I did exactly what Black told me to do. Before I placed my head on his shoulder, I hit the automatic locks and laid my phone underneath my leg so that I could mash emergency if needed. I thought about Parri's pink gun because we needed it right now like never before. These dudes mean business, deadly business.

"Father, please forgive us, and help us. Send your angels, Lord, that these men become blind when they look our way." I shut my eyes, rode and prayed until Black stopped the car. My eyes popped opened, and I was terrified.

"Be cool. Act drunk."

I was so scared until I did the crap like a professional. The juiciest grin went across my face, and I started rubbing all over Black's chest and kissing him on his neck while, from the side of my eye, I watched a man with a pistol walking toward the car. Black's foot wasn't pressing on the gas at all, and I didn't understand why because that pistol represented death in a piece of metal. I started shaking, and Black held on to my hand.

The guy who was walking toward the car was wearing a dark T-Shirt along with some tan slacks, almost like he didn't prepare himself to get dirty. The pistol he held in his left hand pointed at us which was basically our stop sign. Black played it cool and rolled down his window, not easily shaken because he was always willing to throw down if he had to do it. I wanted to play dead because driving off wasn't an option. It would have been a dead give-away. Pretending to be creepy and drunk was the agreed upon disguise that I prayed would work.

"Yeah, man?" Black asked.

"What's going on, young blood? These," the man started, tossing his gun around at his side at the houses behind him, "mailboxes don't have numbers on 'em or they all faded. I ain't got no time for all this shit when I got neighbors that can tell me what I need to know. Where's nine nine nine so I can get my ass outta here. Ain't that what she said, Chino?"

"Yeah, she told him that number. Nine nine nine, man, nine hundred ninety nine," the driver called from the vehicle, and I froze for one second until he faced Black again.

"Yeah, that's it. Nine nine nine, some chick named Jeena lives there. Fuckin' bitch took my money. Hey, drunk," he called for me with his gun tilted into the car. Black remained silent, obviously trying to get us on the good side of the gun. I felt him tensing, just in case he had to fight the gun from the guy's hands and take off which, again, wouldn't have been a good idea. Imagining the car riddled with bullets put me in full acting mode.

I didn't speak back to him after he called me but glanced up at him with a wobbly head and weakened eyes, and that was when he continued speaking, "You know anyone around here named Jeena?"

Tossing my hair from my eyes, I just repeated my name out loud, "Jeena," and started laughing, "What a stupid name!"

"That bitch don't know shit. How about you, my man? Jeena ring any bells?"

"No, man, not at all, but the house you are looking for is down the road on the right. That's nine nine nine."

"Thanks, youngster." The man tucked the pistol in his pants, glanced at our car while shaking his head, and headed back to the SUV. Before he even got inside, me and Black were all the way down the road, making the turn to head out of the neighborhood.

There was a shock of silence that filled the car. By the looks of things, we weren't on the way home either. When I peered over at Black, his face was tightened. If I popped a pimple on it, his whole face would fall to pieces. With my eyes back on the road, I decided to speak.

"She told them my name, Black."

"Shut up, Jeena."

"But, Black..."

"I'm already to my limit, so shut up. I'm staying calm, but I'm tired, Jeena. Did you hear what he said?"

I heard it loud and clear. He said my name. The dude from the SUV with the pistol ready to kill said my name, and he had to have gotten my name from Tanya, the so-called friend I was running around thinking I was helping. She'd flipped on me early on in the game, and she wanted me to give my life for the money she wanted.

"Yes, Black." My heart sunk, and my feet wanted to run and make me disappear from his face. "I'm sorry," I quivered, and the longer I sat there, the more furious I got with Tanya. What I wanted to do was snatch her out of that hospital bed and beat her down.

"Your girl Tanya set you up. How about that?" He slammed his hands against the steering wheel so hard that I thought it would break. We got set up over your over anxiousness to help her. They know what the car looks like, Jeena. There isn't a car like it in the city! We're riding around with bitch ass on the doors of the car!"

"Where are we gonna go?"

"Not home, Jee. Their road goons just got arrested over at our place. They just don't know that you live there, Jeena. I'm gonna stop by my boy's garage and have him paint this ride, paying him with some of this money, so I can pick it up in two days. There was no way he didn't memorize our faces, and when they get to the house, it's gonna be empty. Your friend Tanya really did it to you...to us. We're stuck with the evidence. Looks like she wanted you to get the money before they got there."

He decided to go to his mechanic friend's house he called Half-a-Dime. Half-a-Dime because he would give Black a cut for any work he did for him on his car because they go way back. This was one of those times where Half-a-Dime was going to have to push Black to the front of the line.

"Are you gonna tell him what's up?" I asked.

"No. And you keep your mouth closed, too. I'm gonna tell him to keep the car covered, not to let it be seen until all the paint is removed. I'm gonna have to pay him double for this because he may have to refund someone for not having their car finished because of me. We'll see. We're taking a cab back home, after we dump this money off at Tanya's hospital room and tell her off."

My hands started to quiver, not from fear, but because I felt that I could break her nose off with my fist. Who else would have known what to tell those goons back there but Tanya? She wanted me dead? Did she really want me dead? I couldn't even get sad. That emotion was gone. The only thing I felt was slap down, and she was gonna get it inside that hospital. "And then, I'm gonna turn her ass in." Yeah, I said it.

"Don't do it so fast. Turn that recorder on... no! Make it the video. You ask her questions and then read her response out loud. Get her whole story when you tell her you got the bags. Don't tell her I went with you, and when you secure her story on the recorder, call me, and then I'll alert the law to tell them that the men who were at the house wanted this money, drug money. I'll take the money to the police while you secure that story by prompting it. Done deal, and it sets us free. Tired of this crap. She almost got us hooked on a felony and killed."

"Cool. I'm..."

Black cut me off. "I'm sorry, too. We pulled each other into mess, but this is the last time or we're gonna have to do some serious thinking about moving out of the country."

I touched his hand, and he squeezed mine. "I love you. We're gonna get through this one together, just like we have all the rest. All things work together for the good..."

"For those who love the Lord!"

"Don't even get mad, Jeena. Just put the truth out so that it can set us free. Where's your sister?"

"I don't know. She might still be at the hospital."

"Call and check. She can be a witness, and she..."

"No, I don't want her involved. I like the original plan." I was amped. If I could have reached through time, I would have knocked Tanya out. She must have given them my name when they had her hemmed up in the bathroom cutting her throat. Sure, name drop, but not mine! And then to send me over to the house to collect money after the name drop so that they are looking for me because they know that I would have the money? That was nothing but a set up, and I was crushed, but not as crushed as I wanted her skull for what she did to me.

"I need to pray, Black." I put my head down onto my knees and started to thank God for saving our lives. Then, I asked Him to take the hurt and anger away from me that I was feeling toward Tanya because He put me on the better end anyway. I wasn't the one with my throat slit. Then, I thanked Him for not delivering me into the hands of who I now knew to be my own personal Judas the backstabber with a wig. I then prayed that when I entered Tanya's room, I had the ability to not do anything illegal that would land me in prison for thirty. I ended with an Amen.

When I raised my head, it sunk in that Tanya was never really my friend. She loved money more, and the love of it was the root of all evil. I imagined myself shot to death, me and my unborn baby along with Black, behind her bull. How could she just end my life like that with no thought, or tell me about what she said to them while I was standing there with her in the hospital room? My mind was in such a fog until I just found comfort in God for getting us out of the valley of the shadow of death while rubbing my stomach.

We finally got to Half-a-Dime's garage slash house, and Black being paranoid about calling him from the cell phone, didn't do so on the drive there just in case. He didn't want Half-a-Dime dragged into court later over his paint job in case something crazy popped off. That was understandable. Black was a guy who looked out for his people, and this was a close friend. Therefore, we walked up to the door and knocked. Half-a-Dime came to the door with wake up all in his eyes, and his face was a total wreck, just like the mangled cars he rebuilds.

"Hey, man, what's up? You alright?" Black asked.

"Back up a bit, Black. I think I got the flu, man, or something. I've been resting all day, but I feel much better than earlier. Must be a twenty four hour virus or something. What's up? Hey, Jeena."

"Hi," I replied, backing all the way from the door and into the grass. I wasn't about to catch the bug.

"I need a favor, and I have triple the money to get it done fast. Forty eight hours tops."

"I got you, bro. Tell me about it."

"I need the car repainted. You remember Milanje?"

"Yeah, what about her."

"She got shot to death in my house in my bedroom after she spray painted my car all around, even the tires."

"Word?"

"Like the scriptures, man, like the scriptures."

"You on the run, man?"

"No, HD, man. She tried to shoot me and Jeena, but ended up shooting Jeena's friend Parri. The cops came and let us go because it was self defense when Parri shot her, and then Jeena went right behind her and shot her again making sure she was dead."

"No shit," he yawned.

"Can you knock that out for me?"

"Yeah, I'll hit it later on, around about one in the morning. Take that paint off. By daybreak, start the coats."

Black handed him the money, and Half-a-Dime grabbed him by his shoulder. "What's this? All this cash, money? You know I look out for you. No sweat."

"No, HD, I need it fast is all. This time, I have to square you away."

"As fast as I can get it to you. You're riding around in a clown car, man. And you know me, I got no questions to ask you, bro."

"I need to get a cab now, man. I'm in a hurry."

"No, no, Black. You know I got three cars. Lemme get you the keys, man. I know you're good. Hold up." When he got back to the door, he had the Lysol in one hand, and he sprayed the keys down until they were soaked. "Hold that up for about thirty seconds, and then take the black car with the rims over there."

"Thanks, Half-a-Dime."

"You know I got you."

They knuckled up with a pound, and Black and I left in the rimmed up, black mustang with Tanya's pile of crooked money in the back. When Black started up the car, it was loud and so wrong for the occasion, but we would make it work because it was the only choice we had. Beggars couldn't be choosers.

"I like how you gave him one part of the story."

"That's all he needed to know until we know that we're in the clear. We have to do this because if Tanya really did what we know she did to us, she could pay someone to off us with that kind of money back there. Can't trust her, so we have to nail her. Just go with your gut in there, Jee."

"I can't go with my gut because my flesh will grab her and shake her until those stitches and glue come loose from her old dirty neck. And, Black, I had all her blood all over me, and she's gonna send me to die for this flippin' money!" I grabbed some money out of the bag and tossed it out of the window.

"Jeena, calm down!" He looked out the rearview window, and I looked out the side. We both watched as people on the street ran to it like it was the last cash on the planet. Times were hard. We started to laugh. That felt good. I almost felt like Robin Hood, in the female sense.

I waited until Black left with all the money to take it to the cops before I went inside the hospital escalator. The plan was to tell the cops the truth about everything…that she sent us to the house to get the money, tell the cops that we think that it's drug money, and then we say who sent us with a key to get it while she was planning our death all along. It was about to be a done deal. I was to call Black when it was all done so he could do his thing, but he wouldn't enter the police station without the proof.

"Lord, please be with me. I was just trying to help. Please forgive me…and forgive Tanya." I was angry, but I still loved Tanya, much more than she loved me. I'd proved that one stupidly. That wasn't going to stop me from bagging this one. She tried to get me killed, and now I have to set myself free, hoping it didn't backfire.

The elevator ride was long. I wanted to stop and check on Parri, but I knew I wasn't allowed back yet. It wasn't time for visitors back in ICU. Therefore, I was on my way to Tanya's floor in hopes that she was completely alone.

The elevator stopped, and I walked off, taking a pause. There as a very small waiting area in front of me, but there wasn't a sign of Ms. Bell or the kids. I turned right and started walking, hitting the button to make the corridor's heavy double doors come open. Staring me in the face was the nurses' station, but they paid me no attention. The security guard at Tanya's door saw me from down the hallway and moved his chair from in front of the door. My name was on the list. She was still under protection, not as heavy, but still protection until tomorrow. Since Tony was deceased, there was really no real connection, so the word was that they were going to release the guard from guard duty, at least that was what the nurse said when I left the hospital on the way to get the cash for Tanya.

Nodding as I walked into the room at the guard's go, I first spotted Tanya's feet poking up out from underneath the cover. No one was in the room with her, and I'd already zoomed in on the window where I would lean my phone so that the video would catch me reading her notes she writes back to me in reference to the money she asked me to get.

"Hi, Tanya!" I stated ecstatically as I hit record on my video. Tanya was just waking up and that was great for me because while she wiped her eyes off, I quickly and inconspicuously placed the cell phone at the proper angle and then sat down on the chair pretending that something was in my shoe.

At first, she stared at me, kind of like she'd seen a ghost. Then, she grabbed the pen and pad beside her bed, wrote back the word hi in big bold letters, and then held it up. Great, I thought! I continued with the conversation, placing my shoe back on.

"Here is the key to the house back. When I got there, the door actually broke, like it has termites or something, but me and Black got it back on the hinges for you. We also found the bags you asked us to pick up." I handed her the key to the house, and she squeezed it across her heart. Then she started to write again, and I was prepared to read it out loud. After she wrote, I took it from her fingertips. It read *Was my money all there?*

"Yeah, yeah, Tanya, money was in there. I don't know how much was supposed to be there because all you told me was two bags. There was a lot though... enough to take care of you and the kids, so explain to me what happened, Tanya. What kind of money is this, Tanya, drug money, murder money or what because there's a lot and I'm not used to that. It's not how I live."

She started to write again, and she wrote the whole story from beginning to end on the paper. It took her about ten minutes, and when she finished, I took the sheet of paper from her and read it as I sat down with my back turned to my cell phone video. The paper was held up in the air high enough that she couldn't see my eyes reading, but the camera could capture all that was written. I was just that close to the camera. It read:

"Tony had drug money. He brought a load of money into the apartment, and he told me that it was so full that they wouldn't even know that it wasn't all there and that he'd taken the rest of the money he owed and added to the stash at his old place which is really our place now that I have a key. That's the place that I sent you to. When he called the lifters to retrieve the money he was supposed to supply them with, they came, but turns out they got there before I left the house, so I had to stay. Jeena I was scared."

I flipped the paper over and continued to read.

"After Tony gave them a load of money, they made him spread it out, so they could pack it in briefcases. I knew there would be trouble then, so I shunned my kids back into the room and shut the hall door. Long story short, they had enough cases for more money and it didn't fill up. That's when things went wrong, and I mean dead wrong. Tony said that the rest of the money was in the balcony storage room. They followed him over there, and when he came back inside, I noticed he had a toy box. He really didn't have the money, so I stood up from the chair. Tony looked up and bolted out the door when one guy put his gun *down. That left me. The other guy chased him, but you know Tony, fast as lightening. (By the way, rip this up and scatter it when you're done)."*

She handed me another sheet as I placed the first piece of evidence on the floor. This would prove that I had no idea about what was going down. I continued to read.

"When the other man who was chasing Tony came back, both him and the other guy dragged me down the hallway, and I saw my oldest looking out through a crack. He then shut the door back and locked it. Girl, I was fighting like a mad woman! They kept kicking me and asking where the money was, and I didn't tell them squat. Then they unloaded on me again and put a knife to my throat. I still kept my lips shut because I knew that if I lived, I would have more money that I would ever need to take care of myself and my kids. I never had that much money in my life, and I was dead set on getting it. They slit my throat, left, and that's when I called Parri for help. Damn the cops and damn death. That money was gonna be mine. You guys came, and now I'm here."

I placed the paper down on top of the rest of them and watched her slowly shuffle herself onto her side a bit. I couldn't help myself. I had to ask her.

"Tanya," I started and then paused. Taking another deep breath, I then stated, "I see what you wrote and all, but why didn't you tell me all this when you asked me to get those bags from the house?" I was still setting up my freedom with that question. All she did was shrug her shoulders and put her hands up in the air. I took that to mean that she didn't know. "Don't you think that's something you should have told me?"

Frustrated, she picked up the paper again and started to write. The paper said:

"It was nothing. I have a key to the place, and I just needed you to go grab some bags for me or I would be stuck with nothing, Jeena. You were safe. I see you didn't get hurt, mangled or killed. Be happy!"

I sat there and thought about it as I read the paper. Tanya wanted me dead, didn't she? I recalled the conversation I had with her the other day when she told me about Tony being a drug dealer and having tons of money while she was gonna get her hands on it, and I was the only one who knew the so-called plot. She never wanted me to tell a soul because it would put her on the line. She told those gangsters my name on purpose. She told them that I stole the money! If they killed me, then she would get away totally free with all that loot. The goons would think they got vengeance, but something still didn't make sense. How would she have gotten the money she sent me to get if they'd killed me while I was in the house and snatched the money at the same time? She would still be on the losing end with no money.

I sat there and thought about it. It didn't take long for me to think of the only other thing that would benefit her from ratting me out as someone who stole the money.

"There's more money isn't there, Tanya?" There had to be. It couldn't be just the money she told me to go get after she led those goons to the same house just to clear her and Tony's debt. There had to be more.

Tanya didn't look up. She continued to fiddle with her sheets, so I stood up and walked over to her. "There's more money, isn't there, Tanya?" I asked, gritting my teeth together so hard that I thought my teeth would buckle. I watched as her breathing began to deepen, and then she reached for the nurse's button. I blocked her and tossed it behind the bed. "Tell me, Tanya, because guess what?" She glanced up hesitantly at me. "Those goons ran into me and Black," I continued, stretching my eyes open like I was talking to a little baby while lightening my voice like she was one. "And they told me that they were looking for me. Too bad you didn't tell them what I looked like, Tanya!" I said in baby talk.

Feeling like I was about to grab her halfway stitched up throat and choke the life from her, I backed up. "You set me up. As a friend, I went to get those bags from the house, and you'd already told them where to find their money so that they would think that was my house and that I'd stolen it! Hell, you even gave me a key to the damn house! Didn't you do that?! Then they would kill me and take those bags of money, huh? They would think they won. But nooo, Tanya, you would get nothing then but your freedom. Is that the reason why they didn't slit your whole throat? You opened your mouth and set me up? There's more money. There is more money, Tanya, so tell me where it is or I'm going for the cops," I said silently.

In tears, Tanya wrote on the paper shakily. When I snatched it from her, I coerced her eyes into following me as I slowly and angrily walked over to the camera that she just realized was on and read it out loud into the mic like I was a radio host. It read:

"I'm sorry, Jeena. Please don't go to the cops, and I'll tell you where the money is. I love you, Jeena, but I never had that much money before. I was set, Jeena. It's in the floor of the same house in the dirtiest room. There's a hole in the corner. I'll split it with you if you forgive me. Your name slipped out, Jeena, and before I remembered, I was sending you over there…I'm sorry."

My name *slipped out*? I stood up along with my cell phone, tears all in my eyes, as I stared at my friend. I remembered when I had her back when she was about to go to jail for stabbing Tony at the beginning of her pregnancy. It was me who held her when she was hurt. It was me who she asked to be her matron…for a fake wedding. It was also me that she set up to be murdered so that she would be set free by the goons. She was going to get out of this hospital and go collect the rest of the money, the real money that she was going to keep for her and the kids, and it was going to be over my dead body - literally.

"You wanted them to kill me, Tanya. You didn't even expect me back, and that's why you looked at me with such shock when I came in the door, huh?" I wiped my eyes and collected the evidence that she wrote from the floor. "I love you, too, Tanya...no, no, don't write anything else," I said quietly as I shoved the paper off of the bed. Then I snatched the pen and threw it up against the wall with all the force I had. "Have a nice life in prison. You might just get life."

Her eyes went crazy, and she tried to lift herself from the bed. As she did it, I caught her before she fell to the floor. Our eyes met, and her breath met my cheek. "Your kids will be fine. I love them far more than you love me." She wouldn't let go of my clothes, so I had no choice but to call out loud to security. He came running in and pulled her off of me as he saw that I wasn't holding her, but it was her holding me.

I left the room. This was the first time since Tanya's attack that I heard her scream. The nurses went running inside the room, and her voice echoed all the way down the hall. I didn't even turn around. Our friendship...

<u>Was Over.</u>

I called Black as I took the stairs, on my way down to the ICU unit. By the second flight of stairs down, I leaned onto the railing. Black answered.

"Black, I did it. I got it on video, sound and all. I also have a confession of the whole thing on paper." I started crying. "Black, she tried to have me killed for money. There's more...in the floor of the house. I was the bait for what the gangsters thought was money I'd stolen. In reality, that wasn't even all the money. There's tons left in the floor of the house. She was going back to get it after I took the fall..."

"Jeena, baby, it's gonna be okay. It's tough, but I know who I married. You may make mistakes, and you may not be the biggest and strongest but you're tougher than any woman I know. She wasn't your friend, Jeena, and if she was, something changed. It doesn't even matter what changed her. The fact is that she tried to have you killed so that she could escape and get over. Now, if you're still down, I'm going into the police office to explain how everything ties together with these bags of money. Meet me up here with the proof."

"Okay, Black. I'm still down," I sniffed. "I'll be there."

"Alright, baby. Let me do this," he said as I heard him opening the door of the car. "Things ain't always what they seem."

"Yeah, they aren't. I'll be right there after I go in to see Parri, my true friend."

"I'm your friend, Jeena. Jesus is your friend. If I ever flip, I'll let you know."

"I love you."

"Always love you, too, babe."

We hung up. I made my way down to Parri's room. It was almost time for visits to begin. I got myself together, getting off one floor above Parri and walked to the elevator because I didn't know if I could get through via the staircase on ICU.

Everything appeared so solemn. I had no one to talk to, and my mind was stayed on Tanya's well being no matter what she'd done to me. I was probably going to never see the kids again once Ms. Bell found out what I had to do to her daughter. As a matter of fact, she would probably slap me in my face while her grandkids kick me in the shin. Who was going to take care of them, all of them, and with what? Ms. Bell couldn't afford it. Just the thought made me numb.

Finally, I reached the ICU unit, and Parri's mom was the first person I saw at the door ready to go through.

"Hi," I said.

"Cheer up, honey. Parri is gonna be fine. I'm her mom, and I look better than you do right now. Don't you feel bad because of this. God is good. You girls have always looked out for each other. I hear the stories. The doctor told me that she's going to be fine. Just fine. Clear those red eyes up." She reached into her purse and pulled out some eye drops. I used them, but she had no idea why my eyes were really red. I wasn't going to reveal a thing.

"Thanks."

"Let's go. She'll be out of here in about another twenty-four to seventy-two hours. She's breathing, and they want to be sure that things are working right before they send her upstairs with Tanya, on the same floor."

I remained quiet, just continued to walk to Parri's room. When we got there, her eyes were open, and she put on a weak, yet sassy, smile with a slight roll of her eyes. Yeah, she was getting better.

"Oh gosh, don't start," I said with a big smile on my face. Her face was the light of my night.

"I'mma get you, Jeena."

"Hush now, Parri!" Her mom interjected. "The doctor said to stay calm and let your body heal. All this morphine they got in here, it's crazy that you're talking now."

I walked over to Parri's side, grabbed her hand and gave her a kiss. "Please, forgive me. I love you, girl, and I can't ever repay you for what you did to save me and Black."

"Thank you for praying for me," she responded at a whisper. "Oh and my pink pistol's pleasure. I'm not a butthole after all, huh?"

"No," I weeped. "You're the best girlfriend I have." My cheek pressed against her cheek, and then I left, leaving her with her mom. I had to go see about Black at the police station. Instead of getting Parri's mom to drop me off, I just...

Caught A Cab.

"Thanks."

"Good night, Miss," the cab driver said as I exited the car. The police station stood before me, and I shrunk in front of it. It seemed overpowering because I was about to turn Tanya in.

216

"Well, here I go." As I walked, Half-a-Dime's car was right there parked at a meter. Things went in slow motion because I never thought that I would end up in a situation where I was locking my friend...or the friend I thought I had...up. It was my life she put at stake, so there were no other options.

Walking through the doors, I didn't know who to speak to or what to do. Things were in such a fog for me mentally that I just stood there completely worn out. Finally, an officer spoke.

"May I help you, ma'am?"

"Yes, uhm, I'm here to meet my husband Black with some evidence," I explained, lifting my cell phone up in the air with the papers.

"His name is Black?"

"Stay...Stay Black."

"Stay Black?"

I groaned. "Yes, Stay as in stay here. Black as in the color."

"Baby, I'm over here."

There he was, showing himself in the midst of my spelling things out for the officer about his name. I was so happy to see him until I just burst into a silent cry. The officer escorted me over to Black, and Black met us halfway.

"Come on. This way. I got her officer. Thanks one million."

The officer tipped his head and left from our presence. Black wrapped his strong arms around me, and I just fell inside them. I'd been strong long enough. I really was glad that I had a husband who loved me. After I caught an emotional breather, I stood back up, and we walked all the evidence over to the desk where the officer sat with all that dang on money. My blood money.

"There's more, officer," I snitched, sitting down beside Black. I have the letters that she wrote to me, and then I have all of it on video. You can see, she wrote it, and she admitted to having me set up to die and take the money. She even offered me half not to come here and turn her in."

"Ma'am, I'll watch this and see. You two have been through too much this past week. I say you should get a set of new friends."

"I'll say that right behind you, doc."

"I just need you guys to fill out some paperwork and other items, download this file from your phone to my computer, take the SD card if you don't mind until I can get it back to you at a later date, and you're free to go. Try to have a good night."

"Are you going to arrest her now?"

"Yeah, we have to go put her on lock down while she's in the hospital."

"What about her kids?"

"They'll be taken care of. Don't you guys worry. Things will be fine."

Black grabbed my hand. "Let's just do this so we can get out of here."

"Sure."

That was it. Black and I did whatever the officer said. We gave statements as to what happened, and then we left the building. As we walked outside hand in hand, we took in the night's air. Then, Black brought my hands up to his chest and bowed his head. I followed. It was prayer time.

"Thank you, Jesus, for this day. Thank you for bringing us out of the trouble and the evil around us because we don't deserve those blessings yet you give them to us daily. Thank you for your mercy and provision. We will always give honor to You. Please forgive us for not treating each other right in anger, but show us how to understand one another more so that in times of anger, we can soothe each other in wisdom and kind words. Father, there is none like You. We worship and praise you, in the name of Jesus, Amen."

"Amen. Thank you, Jesus."

"Now," he sighed, turning to face Half-a-Dime's black mustang on the street. "Let's go home finally."

"Yeah, so we can get ready to have and raise our baby."

"In a new house."

"Heck, yeah!"

"With no murders attached."

"Exactly."

"Did you call Faith and tell her everything that went on with Tanya?"

"She'll figure it out soon enough." Faith was gonna be at the hospital at any moment more than likely. "She's gonna pray for her anyway. We will, too."

"Amen. She needs it. Her and her kids."

We reached the car, and he opened my car door like a gentleman to let me in. My phone rang. As Black got in, he glanced over at my phone.

"Who's that?"

"Speak of the heavens. It's Faith."

"Answer it."

"Hello?"

"Jeena, Tanya's tied down to her bed! She must be going crazy or something because they had to literally tie her down because her sutures were breaking loose."

"Faith," I started, looking over at Black and then told her...

<u>"It Ain't Quite What You Think."</u>

THE END

MORE AKIRIM PRESS BOOKS

Books by Mirika Mayo Cornelius

Secret

Colored Lily: Poppa Took My Innocence

Paton

Ain't Quite What I Thought!

Ain't Quite What I Thought! 2

Sunny Sides of My Shade

Murders at Gabriel's Trails: The Complete 5 Part Series
plus bonus Sins of Bain

Books by Rod Cornelius

Diggin' Gold

The Trusted

Single Again

Ghetto Eyes

The Best Kept Secrets

Ugly

Books by Cyan Deane

Dead Man's Mayhem

Execution's Karma

Preview **Murders at Gabriel's Trials: The Complete 5 Part Series plus bonus Sins of Bain** by Mirika Mayo Cornelius

Alexis spots Bain walking casually down the trail with his confident swag and cell phone to his ear. Whoever he was talking to, Alexis doesn't care. For the most part, she's just ecstatic to see that he is coming up the trail to meet her like her knight in shining armor. She trusts him so much until she feels like absolutely nothing can hurt her in the world, including in Gabriel's Trails. Besides that, Bain is well known for his handsomely strong stature and no hesitations when it comes to taking care of any trouble that comes his way. He's never killed anyone, however, but after he's finished dealing with anyone who crosses him, the word is that the victim of his anger wishes Bain had taken his life.

Bain is about six feet two in height, medium build but built into a brown skinned body that any woman would love, including young girl. He has a youthfulness about him that appeals to all the women because although he is all about no nonsense when it comes to what belongs to him, he's also tender and respectful and can make any woman blush, let alone a teenager. It is Alexis that has his heart though, and most ladies know this.

He's finally within arms' reach of Alexis and pauses before reaching out to embrace her. "Why did you walk this far up, Lex? You know I don't let you walk this far up the trail…"

"I'm a big girl, babe," she responds, tip toeing to plant him a kiss on the lips while he stands there and takes it all in, rubbing the small of her back like he wants to undress her on the spot. The trail is lined by trees on both sides, and as Bain pulls back from the kiss, he gently turns her backwards so that she can see why coming this far into Gabriel's Trails is dangerous.

224

"Do you see the main road anymore, Lex?"

"No, Bain," she drags.

"Nothing but a trail that ends, curving back into where you came from. Nobody can see you anymore, Lex. At that point," he explains, pointing to a boulder that's painted red on the side of the trail, "Coming in here beyond that rock this far up means that you're on your own." He turns her back around so that he can look her in the eyes. "I don't ever want you to be on your own, Lex."

"Like I said, I got me."

Preview **SECRET** by Mirika Mayo Cornelius

"I told you your aunt is resting, didn't I?"

I reach my leg back and kick him in his mouth. He yanks his head back and stares at me like he's gonna kill me, so I kick him again with both of my legs swinging like a wild bat. He jumps on top of me holding my right leg with his hand and ducking away from my other leg while its kicking. He starts to unbuckle his pants with his other hand.

"Yeah, it's present time now. You done asked for it. I heard about your momma. A nice piece of work there."

He rips off my pajamas after he gets his pants down. My heart fills up with scary feelings when I just now figure out why my Aunt May said what she told me all the time. Where's Aunt Janie?

"Aunt Janie! Your friend is in my room! He's not supposed to be in here, Aunt Janie!" I yell the loudest I can yell.

Sam reaches back with his right hand and hits me on the side of my stomach. I curl up in a ball.

"Guess what, Secret. She ain't coming so ain't no use in you calling for her. You act like I'm about to hurt you. I wouldn't have hit you like that if you didn't try to wake up your aunt, so I'm sorry. Now hold still."

He feels up my back with his naked hand. My stomach is aching. He keeps acting like he ain't gonna do nothing to me, but this don't feel right. I keep thinking about Aunt May while his hand is going up my leg. I feel something wet on my leg, too. I yank away, but he jerks me in front of him. Jesus, please, help me, Lord. Tears are falling every which way down my face, but then I see it. I fell asleep with my pencil beside me in my bed. It's halfway covered up with my sheets.

"Touch it."

I look back at him, and he closes his eyes.

"Look down and touch it."

That's when I look down and see what he's talking about.

I panic.

"Get off of me! No! I'm not touching that thing-ever! What is that? Aunt Janie, please!" I reach for the pencil real fast, but I don't know what to do with it yet. My hand grips the pencil like somebody else got it for me. My other hand grabs that long, ugly thing, and my hand, with the pencil in it, reaches all the way back and stabs that big, ugly thing right in the center.

He lets out the loudest holler I ever heard from a man in my life, and his eyes fly open. I jump up off the bed, and run towards the other end of my room. I look back at his ugly thing and see that the pencil is still stuck in there while he's tumbling around on the floor. His hands are around it, but he ain't pulling it out. It's hurtin' him so bad that I pick up my lamp so that I can aim for his head so I can bang some more pain into him. He justa hollering. Betcha he won't come in my room no more.

Preview **Diggin' Gold** by Rod Cornelius

She wanted him just as bad as he wanted her, but just not bad enough to get it on in the car. She also realized that another round with Trent meant another day of lying to Jimmy, but what he doesn't know wouldn't hurt him, she thought. Besides, she was trying to come up and Jimmy's stock was falling fast. Trent had tangible assets, and she was almost ready to go all in.

"I told you earlier that I had a lack of patience for you. Now how about let's get up out of this ride and take a no-holds barred tour of my humble abode. There won't be a piece of furniture off limits. I promise," he said as he continued feasting on her neck.

She observed his house again, "I don't know if you got a back strong enough for the kind of tour that you're talking about. Your place looks like it has a lot of ground to cover. It could take the whole night to get it all."

He pulled up and backed away from her. "There's only one way to find out."

"Then why are we still in your Jag?"

He backed away further with a smile as she smiled right back at him. "Baby, it ain't nothing but a word."

"Then what are you waiting on?"

"Shiiiiiit!" he said. She finally told him what his ears had been waiting all night to hear. The green light was lit. He knew he could have pretty much any woman he set his sights on but Kizzy carried an extra spiff. Not only was she sexy and a freak in between the sheets, but she was Jimmy's lady. She was the last thing he could take from Jimmy and that was worth more than its weight in gold.

He quickly hopped out of the automobile and danced around the vehicle to open her door. He grabbed her hand to assist her on her exodus. He shut the door, not releasing her hand as they made their way to his front door.

As she stood behind him, she looked up and admired the huge brick home. She had never been in a house as big as his, and she couldn't wait to serenade it with him. "This really is a nice place, Trent. I could see you making me some pancakes in bed here," she joked.

"Oh we 'bout to make something, but it's not going to pancakes, that's for sure." He pulled her into the dark house and slammed the door shut. Then he pulled her into him and gave her a passionate kiss.

"So I guess you mean business," she said as she pulled away from his lips and rested her arms around his neck.

"Do I?" he smiled. He placed both hands on her rump and gripped it tightly, pulling her up off of the floor as she wrapped her legs around his waist. As his tongue ran its slow, slippery course up and down her neck, he walked her through the dark living space and carried her to the leather couch. He laid her down and his tongue twirled around her bosom as his hands made their way down her legs as he began to inch her dress upwards.

Preview **Dead Man's Mayhem** by Cyan Deane

What the hell was that? If they don't get their little southern asses out of my viewing! Rest in peace? Mary made my life a living, breathing, stinking hell, and she has her sweaty panties coming in here trying to start some real shit while I'm still trying to wake myself up from this doomsday nightmare.

Mary – she's the lady that built the straw house that I wanted to crap on each and everyday to make that thing fall down right on top of her ass. When I would walk into her bar, for some reason or another, she would always be there. What owner is always at their establishment? That's the purpose of hiring people to work for you while you sit your ass at home and play golf in the middle of lunch time traffic so everyone can see what a grand life you have. She would make her baggy eyeballs twitch at me, and she's only forty one years old, looking and sounding like a grandma of eight hell raisers.

Truth be told, Mary would constantly talk shit, but it was shit that I could never hear. Call me paranoid, but she was ten words from getting popped in her mouth the day I supposedly went cold. I still don't even know who knocked me over my damn head in her nasty ass bar, but I swear it was probably her ass that set me up. She hated me, and I could tell. Her raggedy bar wasn't even that good for anything, but I was determined to go inside each and every week to make her life-long dream of store ownership reek of irritation with my presence.

I'd come to find out that I dated Mary's second cousin, Barbara Sue, back in the day for like three minutes tops, and Barbara Sue had gone and told her whole felon ass family that I was the one who broke her heart into pieces. First off, what they didn't know was that I would have never dated anyone seriously named Barbara Sue. Let's get that out there right now.

Secondly, all I did was kiss her after talking on the phone with her for about one week.

When I met up with her, Barbara Sue wasn't really my type, but hell, the date was still on. We went to see a movie, parked it at the park, kissed and I took her snaggle toothed mouth home. It's true I never called again, but it was a damn shame how she ran my name in the mud about it.

Preview **Single Again** by Rod Cornelius

"Hey, do you have a name?" She didn't answer. She blatantly ignored me, just like she did when I first approached her in the club. Now see, it's things like that, that makes a man think with his brain and not his jimmy all of the time. But then I took another glance at her body and quickly realized how much more powerful a man's jimmy is than his brain. As a matter of fact, it is his brain. Besides, this chick was a perfect ten. A ten, then some. And those are just too hard to come by at times.

Her directions led me straight to a two-story brick house smack-dab in the middle of Brenton Avenue. "Keys," she chillingly requested. A brief thought of being stranded in the middle of nowhere swiftly raced through my mind. I gave her the keys. "Come on," she said. Thank you, Jesus. I couldn't bare the thought of walking all the way back to that club and trying to quickly compose a lie to Rex as to why I was perspiring so badly.

I jumped out of the car and shadowed her tracks like a starving dog sniffing for a meaty bone. She opened the door to the house and flicked on the lights beside the entrance. As I stepped into her crib, I began to instantly think that this experience had to be some kind of cruel joke sponsored by my subconscious and somehow, I was sleeping and couldn't wake up. And the way it was beginning to feel, this was gonna be a wet one.

She glanced back at me, "Close the door." I shut the door and followed her up the stairs. The house really didn't have much in it. In fact, it looked unlived in altogether. The walls were neatly entangled with an assortment of oil paintings but not much furniture consumed the home. Nonetheless, my primary concern rested on just one piece of furniture in particular the bed!

We walked into what had to have been the master bedroom. It was humongous. An exquisite Persian rug laced the floor. There was a huge floor-length window open, and the nightly breeze blew her finely-silk draperies into the room. Most

232

significantly of all, she had this massive king-sized bed in the center of the room.

I looked around, not trying to seem overly-amazed. "So this is yours?"

"Nope!" she said as she walked alongside her bed, slowly sliding her fingers across the satin sheets.

Damn! I knew she had to have a man, somewhere.

"Well, it is for now. My agency is leasing this place for me until I find some place to live down here," she said.

"Oh," I said relieved that there was no sign of any manly presence in her life so far. "All this for you, huh?"

She grinned. "Yeap."

I walked over to the window and gazed down at the dimly lit street. I didn't want to seem too anxious for what she had to offer. "Nice view."

"I'll say," she replied.

I could almost feel her eyes cutting through my back. I turned around, thinking maybe I could slip a little bit of my own arrogance in there. "I was referring to the street."

"I was, too. What else would I be referring to?"

Ooh, low blow, and can't say that I didn't deserve it. As she took a seat on the bed, I just stared at her, not having a clue to where things were headed. But if I knew anything, I definitely had to have them go the direction I wanted them to.

"So," I took a deep breath. "Why did you bring me here?"

"Why did you come?" she quickly combated.

"What? You grabbed my hand and led the way."

"You're a grown man. I'm quite sure you could've stopped me."

www.ingramcontent.com/pod-product-compliance
Lightning Source LLC
Chambersburg PA
CBHW070105260626
47160CB00004B/1322